WAITING FOR THE PIECES

TAYLOR WILSON-WEST

Paperback ISBN: 979-8-9883969-6-3

eBook ISBN: 979-8-9883969-7-0

Cover Design by Indie Editorial, LLC

Edited by Trinity McIntosh, Type A Tweaks

Proofread by Tina White, Ashley Depointe

Formatted by Taylor Wilson-West

WAITING FOR THE PIECES

Dedication

To all of my thriller babes who need a little romance too.

AUTHOR'S NOTE

Hello party people, if you've picked Waiting for the Pieces up, welcome! I'm so excited you're here. This is not my usual brand of sweet and steamy, this book is twisted and sometimes crude and graphic.

Some content to be aware of:

Death of a loved one

Graphic depictions of torture (including genital mutilation)

On page murder

Sexually explicit scenes

Consensual-nonconsent

Exhibitionism

Voyeurism

Degradation

Praise

Stalking

As always, I strive to be as transparent as I can by giving you these warnings, however I am human, so if I missed one, please let me know, and I will correct it as soon as possible.

Now, buckle up, buttercup.

You're in for a ride. (:

They circle each other, like birds of prey.
Until he has no choice but to send her
away.
It is the hardest thing he's ever had to do.
But he can no longer sit by while she turns
blue.

Chapter One

H e's late... *again.*

I swear that man would be late to his own funeral with the way he cares for time. Everyone here though, they would still cheer as his casket made the trek down the aisle. He was Manson Hayes, the great and wonderful.

The soiree our mother insisted on, is one for the ages. Anyone who is anyone got an invite.

The only reason I'm here is because the golden boy himself is my brother. Yes, biologically. Though you wouldn't know it looking at us. Where he's tall, I'm short. He's slim and well muscled, and I'm thicker around the midsection. He is beautiful and I'm less...in-your-face pretty. Just your average, lovely, dark haired angel, our dad says.

It's not like I think I'm ugly or anything. My nose is straight, without plastic surgery, my lips are full and shapely, and man did God really give me the best tits a girl could ask for. High, and perky, and more than a handful. I've always thought I was a knockout.

Manson oozes confidence, no matter what he is doing, it's his superpower. Speak of the devil and he shall appear. He walks through the front door with a big grin on his face, showcasing the natural straight pearly white of his teeth.

His blue eyes are so bright against the beginning of his summer tan. He scans the crowd of his colleagues and our family's closest friends until those bright blue eyes land on my hazel ones.

He makes a beeline for me. I stand with our parents looking like the perfect family, and we are, for the most part. Our dad is the Mayor of our small town, Gravity Hill, and our mother is the biggest socialite. She leads all of the school functions, every ladies night out at the country club, and heads every committee on this side of the state line.

Manson wraps his arms around my shoulders, squeezing me to his chest, "Well, Ferny, I finally did it huh?"

I shove him off me, laughing at his insinuation that he wouldn't be opening his own practice. Valedictorian of his class, and president of the debate team, he graduated a semester early. Manson was always an overachiever, so working for someone else wasn't going to be enough for him for long.

"You smell like women's perfume." I complain, because his latest hook-up is right behind him, and I have hated her since freshman orientation. *His* freshman orientation. Stella Briggs has had her sights set on my brother forever, despite him never paying much attention to her. It's been years since college, and she is still following him around. I'm just glad this will be the last we see of her, with Manson finally leaving TWTM Counseling and Psychology, she has no reason to shadow him like a stalker anymore.

I just finished my PhD in Literacy at Cardis University—at nearly twenty-six years old—I feel pretty accomplished, and our mother simply had to throw a party to celebrate.

Stella sneers over his shoulder as our mother grabs Manson by his biceps and hauls him to her chest. Placing a gentle kiss on both of his cheeks.

"My baby boy," she croons, tears lining her eyes. Manson is close to thirty-two years old for God's sake, but to mom he will always be her baby.

Gag me.

Her nails are bright red against Manson's trim, dark beard. Her hair perfectly styled in beachy waves. Gray streaks almost professionally throughout her dark tresses. Only our mother would grow gray hair damn near perfectly.

Dad slaps Manson on the back and offers him a

lowball glass with a few splashes of whiskey, "My son, the Psychiatrist, branching out on his own."

Manson blushes, as he always does when our father gifts him compliments. His cheeks turn a subtle shade of pink. Almost unnoticeable to others, but not me. My brother and I are best friends. Well, as much as we can be.

I still have my secrets, and the biggest one just walked through the door.

Awareness prickles the hair on my arms, sending shocks of goosebumps over my flesh. Creed Hemlock lights up all of my senses, and has since Manson brought him home for the first time when I was eight.

I didn't understand attraction then. How could I, when the most *manly* man I knew was my father, and I certainly have never been attracted to him.

Creed walks in with the swagger of a well built man. His shoulders thrown back, solid arms hanging by his sides, legs toned and lean. But his face is set in a permanent scowl when he isn't hamming it up for some one night stand, or laughing at my brother. He wears his beard a little scruffy after he found out women preferred his dark facial hair this side of just unkempt, making him look rugged like that cowboy on Yellowstone girls go nuts over.

He nods in my direction when Manson hollers for him

to come over. His eyes lingering on me for just a few more seconds than normal.

I swear he's known about my crush for years, and is waiting on the right time to out me to my brother.

"Hey, man!" Manson shouts over the crowd. They did everything together, until Creed left for New York. He's been gone on and off over the past three years, and I swear Manson gets lonely when Creed isn't around.

"Doc," he says, a small smile gracing his lips. I look away before I get that stupid look on my face like every other woman in this room. "Thank you for inviting me Mr. and Mrs. Hayes."

Always such a gentleman, even though I've seen a different side of him on the odd occasion that Manson would invite me out with them.

"You know we wouldn't think about celebrating without you, you're like our second son," my mother chirps, her eyes full of genuine love. It's true, he is basically a surrogate son to my mom and dad. He lived with his mother, but every summer he disappeared for a few weeks, presumably to spend with his dad.

Now, he lives at his mother's house when he's here, and who knows where when he is in New York.

I'm not even one hundred percent sure what his family

does for a living. I just know they're loaded, and his older brother hasn't done too bad for himself either.

"I appreciate that," he slaps a hand on Manson's back in one of those bro hugs I have seen one too many times.

"Well, honey. We should mingle." My mother lays her hand on my fathers forearm, and guides him toward the crowd of onlookers while he mouths, "Help me." Mom swats his shoulder playfully before they disappear into the crowd.

"Welp," I start, "I should get going." I ball my hands into fists, pointing my thumbs in the direction of the front door.

"And where are you going?" Manson fires off.

Overprotective brother alert.

"Out with Candy," it's all I was going to give him, and he knows it by the way he locks his fists together in front of his body. It's his tell that he isn't happy. I have been stuck with our parents all day, and I just want to relax.

To unwind with my friends and maybe get laid. He should know it's not easy to find the time to fuck around when you're working toward a PhD, I deserve this.

I *need* this.

"Come out with us tonight," he offers, knowing that it's a tempting suggestion. I would usually jump at the chance, but I've been in a dry spell for months, and if I go out with them I know I will embarrass myself, and definitely Creed too.

I need to get laid if I am going to be spending time with them anytime soon.

"And watch you try to hook up with someone all night? Thanks, but I'd rather stay in, than suffer through that."

"Hey!" He shouts and pulls me closer, "I never have to try *too* hard."

I push away from him, and practically scream, "Gross!"

Manson laughs, and I try my hardest not to look at Creed who is either smiling, or watching us with thinly veiled irritation. Either way, I can't look because if I did, I would probably try to climb him like I've wanted to for years.

I turn quickly, racing up the stairs to change and get the hell out of here. Feeling what I hope are Creed's eyes on me the whole way.

Chapter Two

I lean against my bedroom door, panting from the exertion of running up the grand staircase of our house. The dark wood is a blur in my rush to get away from everyone downstairs.

Yes, I still live with my parents, but in my defense it just made the most sense. I'm not in a relationship and I spend nearly all of my time either at school, studying, or sleeping. There wasn't any rush for me to move out on my own.

My dark purple curtains are thrown open. Big paneless windows lined one whole side of my room, revealing the dusky sky. The sun has barely set over the pine tree tops. A beautiful night for a little debauchery.

Candace has been my best friend since we were in diapers. She's sitting on my bed, her long legs draped over the side, waiting. I have been calling her Candy since we could talk. Mostly because I couldn't say Candace when I was little. Then it just stuck.

Much to my mothers dismay, Candy lives in the trailer park on the outskirts of town. Her dad lost everything they had in a gambling den and her mom left not long after he showed no signs of changing.

But he did change, albeit slowly, and even though he doesn't have much, he gives everything he can to Candy. It's a different type of love, and I find it interesting. Mr. Hayworth hasn't once treated me differently, even after my mother found out who he was, and started trimming our playdates short. Or stopping them all together.

"You said *maybe an hour*," she gripes playfully. She's probably scrolled on her phone, or tried on all my shoes while she has been waiting a few minutes past the hour I said it would take.

"Manson doesn't want us to go," I say and shrug. It's nothing new that Manson doesn't want me going out, he practically hounded me all through grad school.

"Boooooo," she crows as a knock comes at my door. She giggles and hops up, reaching for the door. She turns the knob but I hold firm against the door.

"I don't think that's a good idea," I whisper.

Her eyebrows shoot up and her lips curl into a knowing smile, "*He's* here."

I shake my head, even though she knows I'm a liar,

"Please," I almost beg. I'm not above it.

"This is too good. Maybe now you can tell him how much you wanna ride his big cock until you spray your juices all over him!" She starts moving her hips and laughing at my rapidly reddening face.

"Candy!" I whisper-shout, praying whoever is on the other side of that door didn't hear a filthy word she's saying. My skin heats and the fine hairs on my body lift.

"Fern?" I hear Manson on the other side of the door, "Who are you talking to?"

Candy uses my surprise against me and pulls the door open a crack.

"Hi hot stuff, miss me?" she croons, leaning suggestively against the door frame. Her white t-shirt is ripped from base, to right under where her bra sits, in strips. Jeans covering her from her belly button to her sock feet.

"You know I did, little Candy Cane," he replies, using the nickname he knows she hates.

I pull the door open all the way to end the grossness but stop short when I see Creed behind him.

Shit.

"Well, where are we partying tonight?" Manson claps his hands together, still eyeing Candy.

"We were just saying we might stay in instead, watch some

movies. You know, girl time," I lie, and bless her, Candy jumps right in.

"Yeah, lady times and all," she fakes period cramps and Manson takes a step back like he might just catch them.

It takes all I have in me to not laugh.

"Okay, well if you change your mind we'll be over at Brady's," he tells us before saluting Candy with two fingers and turning on his heel. Creed stands there a moment longer before following my brother down the stairs.

"Oh," lifting his finger to tap his nose, he turns back so I can see his profile, "I don't think you could handle my big cock, Charmer."

Candy cackles and all I can do is stand there, mouth open, praying for the ground to open and swallow me up. Because he can't have possibly heard Candy and I talking that far from the door, and how the hell does he know Candy was talking about *him?*

"If I wasn't already in love with your brother, I'd take Creed up on his challenge," she wiggles her brows.

Candy and Manson are hot and cold with each other, and have been for the past year. I sometimes think if Candy wasn't so free spirited, Manson would be serious about her. She likes to live without restraints, and honestly, with her hand in life, I can't blame her for it.

My brother is about as straight-laced as they come though, and now that his practice is open, he wants to settle down, get married, and have kids.

I sigh, resigned in the knowledge that she would never, ever fuck me over with Creed. She may tease, but she's my person. The vault for all my dirty secrets, tears, and bad deeds.

By the time I allow Candy to do my makeup and dress me like an off-brand Barbie, the party we decided to go to is in full swing. People loitering on the front porch of Dean's family estate. Couples are making out on the lawn, drinks and other party favors flowing. Dean himself gives us a tilt of his cup in recognition before we saunter our way through his front door.

Dean's doing well, a mutual friend of both me and Manson. Taking over his family's business, whatever the fuck it's called, was better for him when he graduated with his bachelors degree. He makes more money throwing parties than most college graduates make in their first year working.

We hooked up in high school and a little while I was at Cardis, but it never meant anything.

I don't date...

"I'm gonna go say hi," Candy wiggles her fingers and I wave her away, already knowing the drill. She will get some sort of contact high while in Dean's presence and come back more handsy than a horny teenager.

I don't mind it. Candy and I are sometimes friends-with-benefits, and we both know it's only for a good time, not a long time. She usually gets her simple pleasures from Manson. But, seeing as he isn't here, my kisses will have to suffice. I think hooking up with my best friend was all the action I got while in school, until I met *him*, the man who checked all my hook-up boxes.

My brother knows Candy and I fool around, but it isn't exactly his favorite subject, so we mostly don't speak of it.

I weave in and out of couples, saying 'hi' when necessary, all while making my way toward the back porch. It's a massive screened-in area where I plan to spend most of my night. Dancing here is cooler than inside, with the late May breeze gently sawing through the mesh.

Gretchen from my freshman dorm sways her way toward me, handing me a cup filled with whatever's on tap tonight,

"Thought you looked a little parched."

I laugh, throwing my head back and feeling my dark hair brush along my spine, "Bullshit." I know her better than that. She wants to know what every woman here wants to know.

'Did Manson come out with you?'

'Is Manson here tonight?'

I learned a long time ago that girls are not my friends.

Candy being the exception. Even though I know she has a thing for Manson, she doesn't flip her whole life around to only hang out with me when he's home. She simply wants to be friends with me.

Gretchen smiles, like I knew she would, and taps her red cup against mine, "To hot older brothers."

"I'm not fucking drinking to that," I say. I don't give a shit if Gretchen's older brother *is* a tall, golden snack. Thinking of anyone fawning over Manson makes me want to puke.

The 'G twins'–Gretchen and Garrett–aren't locals, but they stuck around after Gretchen graduated from Cardis. I'm not sure why, since Garrett only came around because she decided to settle in.

Gretchen meanders through the crowd, laughing as she does, before the golden snack himself makes his appearance.

"Thought I might see you here," he smiles, his mouth a

little too big for his face, but still handsome in a surfer way. He went to school on the west coast, where they're from, for something to do with acting or whatever, "Though, I don't see your brother." I guess the acting thing didn't work out.

"You wanna fuck him too?" I try and fail hiding my smile behind my cup.

"You're funny," he leans down–because his six foot frame has to with my five foot three body–to whisper in my ear, "But he's not the Hayes I was hoping to fuck tonight."

I place my hand on my heart and lean back against the mesh of the porch, "Well damn, did I win the lottery?"

He beams like he was the real winner here, and safe to say, if I had any inclination to fuck him, he would be. But tonight I have my sights set on another man. One who isn't supposed to be here, and yet, still found his way in.

"Only if you're a good girl," usually that line would have me on my knees to prove just how good I can be, but I've decided I want to be the hunter tonight.

Not the hunted.

I look Garrett straight in his green eyes and laugh, "I can promise you that I will not, in fact, be a good girl tonight. Why don't you sit down and watch a woman work, huh?"

Chapter Three

We lock eyes, my plaything and I.

Him, in his thousand dollar suit, hair styled perfectly, even though he probably just left his office in the city. I have seen him late at night, running his hands through his hair, musing the blond strands. The same office my father works in. Gray and I met last summer in the file room one too many times, and well, one thing led to another, and here we are. Chasing each other around when we both need a release.

I make sure my steps are slow and steady.

Measured.

I watch as his eyes slowly appreciate the view, and what a view I must be. With my thick legs covered in shiny black latex, spiked combat boots glinting against the strobing lights in the house. My red cut off shirt that shows off my soft stomach, allowing everyone to see exactly what they pretend not to crave. I say nothing as I lean into him.

invading his space. Despite the heat of the room he looks fresh, relaxed, as if he has every right in the world to be here tonight. Brushing my chest against his abdomen, I tilt my face up toward his so he's forced to look down at me. Our eyes clash, his dark brown eyes pooling like melted chocolate.

"Swung by your brother's party," he says as he brings one of his strong, soft hands up to my face. He twirls one of my raven locks around his finger, gently caressing my face, "Funny, though. The man of the hour was gone."

He leans in, his mouth barely whispering against the shell of my ear, "You want to play tonight, little secret?"

I barely suppress a groan, because he isn't allowed to have the upper hand tonight. I am going to drive him wild until he has no choice but to fuck me until I can't walk in the morning.

I plaster on my sweetest smile and rub my cheek against his, "Always."

My laugh is light, and I slip away from him and into the crowd. Dodging hands and spilled drinks as I set out to find Candy, just to make sure she's alright. Feeling Gray's eyes on me as I do.

He will watch, until he can't anymore.

Garrett's arm sweeps across my shoulders, "So you like

pretty rich boys now?"

I scoff, of course he was watching, he just can't let it go that I don't want to fuck him. I don't reply, instead I allow him to keep his arm there, because I know it will drive Gray wild. Allowing someone else to touch my skin.

He blessedly doesn't say anything else, probably because he knows if I don't want to answer, I won't. Simple as that. His hand draw's idle circles on my back as we stand there while I search the crowd for Candy. I spot a flash of her dirty blonde hair near the front door, she is grinding her hips against Dean's front.

If he was sitting down she would be giving him a fucking lap dance like the highest paid stripper you have ever seen. I laugh, knowing good and damn well she is about to leave poor Dean with the bluest balls he has ever had.

A growl comes from a few feet away as Garrett's hand makes its way toward my ass. I glimpse over my shoulder, finding Gray standing there, face hard and body rigid. But he knows the rules. I will come to him when I want something. I give him a little grin and turn back to Garrett.

He isn't a bad choice to fuck with, his golden skin is practically glowing, and he's a nice enough guy. He'll understand, and then imagine me while he's fucking someone else tonight. The thought makes my smile widen.

"You like making men feral, don't you?" He whispers as I lean up on my tippy toes to face him.

I roll my eyes, because, obviously. Grabbing his shirt and pulling him the rest of the way to me. I know I have Gray's attention, as I devour Garrett's mouth. It makes this ten times hotter.

Yes, I like to be watched. There's nothing sexier than a man willing to watch their partner enjoy pleasure.

Small as this kiss may be.

Garrett surprises me by lifting me by my ass into his arms, he is actually a pretty good kisser, his lips soft, but firm in his movements.

Sure.

Confident.

If there is anything sexier than a man with the confidence to put his hands on my body without restraint, I haven't found it yet.

I wrap my legs around his swimmer's trim waist, practically grinding on his rapidly growing erection. Another surprise, the man had a nice size dick. Not the biggest I've ever had, but not small by any means. I groan when he releases my lips to nip at my neck, and tilt my head to give him better access. I turn and watch Gray's face heat with lust, the brown of his iris has turned almost black with it.

It drives me insane.

Slowly I lift my body up Garrett's, giving him access to my cleavage and it's his turn to groan, "You're gonna kill me, Hayes."

Before he can place his mouth near my chest, I drop down, lining up his now straining cock against my pussy. He gasps, and it is one of the sexiest things I have ever heard. Giving his lips one more good suck, I climb out of his arms, my boots thumping down on the hardwoods. The partiers stop and stare.

"Now, go find yourself someone willing to fuck you, buddy," Garrett's cheeks bloom pink with embarrassment, or amusement, or possibly anger. It's hard to tell with all these endorphins swirling in my head.

I'm sure I look freshly fucked, my lips are swollen, my hair is a mess, and I am fairly certain Garrett bit me hard enough to leave a mark. Gray clocks all of it as I brush past him, making sure that he can feel my hard nipples through the thin fabric of my shirt.

He doesn't make a sound as I pass, and doesn't turn to follow. I guess I'll have to work harder.

Candy finds me, her skin is flushed and she has a big goofy grin on her face, "That was *hot*!" She practically screams.

Her hands land on my face before she leans in and plants

her lips on mine. Kissing my best friend is nothing new.

Hell, Candy practically taught me how to kiss. She takes her time caressing my lips, slowly as if she is memorizing the way they feel, "Business Fucker is staring hard right now," she whispers against my lips.

I smile, feeling her lips follow mine, "I figured as much. He won't wait forever but let's give him a show."

She spins us and slips her tongue into my mouth, her hands squeeze a path down my body. My eyes land on Gray's, his are like liquid fire while his hands ball at his sides. He looks so out of place in his expensive suit. Even though everyone here is in their mid twenties, as a man well into his forties with perfectly styled hair and clothes that cost thousands, he tends to stick out. Candy trails kisses over my jaw, "still watching?" She whispers so only I can hear her.

She is putting on a show, it's been a while since we have done this together. But it's like muscle memory kicks in and I twist my fingers into the strings of her shirt, "Absolutely, along with half the party."

She chuckles, "Good, because your brother just showed up."

Her breath is hot against my rapidly heating skin. If Manson is here, that means Creed isn't far behind.

"Shit."

I hear Manson shouting to some of his friends, and before he can see it's *me* kissing Candy, I twist my head away from where I think he is standing.

Gray disappears into the crowd, knowing he has no good reason to be here, and that if Manson sees him, he will ask questions.

Candy laughs dramatically and turns toward Manson, giving me the perfect cover. I push past the few people lining the way toward the front door. Hoping against all odds that Gray will be out by the road in his Mercedes.

Once the cool May air hits my cheeks I sigh in relief. Manson didn't see me, thank God. That would have been all kinds of fucking awkward, and now Candy can get her handsy on with him.

"Seemed pretty intense with Garrett earlier," I hear a voice say and jump clear out of my skin. I spin and find Dean standing there, smoking something that is definitely not a cigarette. "Whoa, Hayes, jumpy are we?"

"I just needed some air," I stall, waiting for Gray to appear.

I search the cars down the street as lights flash up the hill from Dean's front gates. I spot Gray's headlights as he expertly maneuvers his car to the front door.

A chill runs down my spine and I spin around, watching Dean walk back into the house. Nothing seems out of place, but the hair on my neck stands up. I'm just being paranoid, if Manson sees Gray, he will lose his mind, and tell our father I've been sleeping with his publicist in secret. Not something I want to deal with, I'm a grown woman for fuck's sake.

I rush toward Gray's Mercedes, hopping in quickly like my ass is on fire. Breaths coming in quick pants.

Gray drives for a few minutes, until we are up one of the many mountain passes people park their cars in during the day to start a hike. That is, until he throws the SUV in park and barks at me.

"Get. Out."

With the feeling of being watched still fresh in my mind, all I can do is stare at him.

Chapter Four

"**L**ittle secret, either you get out, or I will fuck you right here in the front seat of my car like a teenager who's finally getting laid for the first time," his eyes are heated, his face hard.

I lean back in the seat and shift my legs open in invitation, and challenge.

"So be it," he says before ripping the seat belt off my body and dragging me over the gear shift into his lap.

"You want to be treated like a two cent slut?" he whispers while I grind down on his obvious erection. He slides his seat as far back as it goes and starts reclining the seat while he works the latex of my pants over my hips. He sucks in a breath when he gets them off and finds me bare. Wetness soaks my skin from being turned on practically since I saw him arrive tonight.

His hands grip my hips in a bruising manner that has me arching my back and moaning out, "Fuck, yes."

He quickly works off my crop top and bra, leaving no room for ceremony. I flip the buckle on his belt and slide it through the loops of his pants I'm ruining with my wetness.

He takes the belt and wraps it around my wrists tightly, tugging it through the 'oh shit' handle in his car. Leaving me hanging, naked and at his mercy. He tilts my body up, gripping my ass in his generous palms and he guides me to his mouth. Swiping his tongue through my pussy with no warning, "God Fern, I could live between your thighs."

I whimper and buck against his mouth, silently begging him to continue. He obliges, running his tongue around my clit in tight circles, sucking hard on the little nub of nerves. He starts up a rhythm, suck, lick, nip. It drives me wild as I grind down on his face as much as I can while also being tied to his fucking car.

"Let it go," he says, his lips brushing my sensitive flesh, "Give me my fucking prize for watching you mouth fuck that surfer boy."

That's all it takes, the reminder of the way he looked at me while Garrett devoured my lips. The orgasm rips through my body like hot fire as he continues to tease and stroke my clit. His hands kneading my ass and thighs.

"I hope you're ready to take my cock, Fern," he says, unzipping his pants and freeing his erection from his tight briefs, "Because *that*, was me being nice."

He lines my body up against the tip of his dick before plunging up while pulling me down in one quick thrust. I cry out at the intrusion, the delicious heat that barrels through my stomach, and the stretch of his fat cock. What he lacks in length he more than makes up for in girth, stretching and filling me up in ways length could never. I move, finding purchase on his leather seats with my boots to match his punishing upward thrusts.

"More," I growl, and he obliges. Sliding one hand over my clit, rubbing hard circles and the other pinching my nipples. We fuck, our skin making the best music as we slap together, harder and harder. Waves of heat pulse through my body. He's working me like a beautiful instrument, and *God* does it feel amazing.

My mind wanders to Creed, imagining he's the one under me at the moment, fucking me the way I like. My walls squeeze and Gray almost slips out in our movements.

"Who are you thinking of when my cock is inside of you?" His voice is breathy with exertion, "Who is it that just made you clench your pussy so hard on my cock?"

I don't answer, I can't. If I do, I'd be the asshole here, imagining another man while I'm taking his cock.

He pulls me off him and twists my body so I'm facing the

windshield. My breasts on full display for anyone walking by to see. He slams into me from behind, sending more flutters of sweet agony through my body. My hands, still hanging on the handle above me, are going numb from the position but I don't care.

"Now, my dearest secret," he begins, punctuating every word with a thrust of his hips, "Think of him while I punish your pussy, and cum like the good little slut I know you are."

My smile is too bright for him not to notice, but this is why I fuck him. He knows I have no feelings for him past the pleasure he can wring from my body, and the same goes for him, "Oh God," I moan as he pushes to a different angle.

As Gray's hands explore and pinch, I imagine their Creeds. His calloused hands roaming over my body, playing the nerves perfectly to get me to the height of pleasure before I fall over the edge. My release sneaks up on me, hard and fast, like Christmas lights erupting inside my head. My orgasm rips through my body, heat flooding my limbs as Gray pulls out and finishes on my ass, never inside.

I lean against the driver's side window, coming down from the high of orgasming twice. Gray twitches behind me, but doesn't make a move to get up so I sit there feeling the aftershocks of our mutually beneficial arrangement.

He cleans up his mess off my ass with the pocket square

from his jacket, then releases the belt around my wrists. Gently rubbing them to get the blood flow back, the buttons of his dress shirt rub against my bare back, the sensation so relaxing, being taken care of.

Not romantically, but respectfully. Gray's the first man I've taken to bed that's done any after care.

It's one of the many reasons I keep coming back for more.

"Lucky guy," he breathes against my neck.

I chuckle, if he only knew, "I'm not fucking him."

"Lucky me then," I can see the reflection of his smile in the front window. It makes me laugh, me sitting naked on his lap, him rubbing soothing circles over my wrists still clothed. We laugh together, yeah, lucky him.

Something catches my attention out of the corner of my eye. A slight wink of light before it's gone.

"Did you see that?"

I ask, pulling myself off his lap and back into my seat. Pulling on my clothes as quickly as I can. Damn leather.

I can see the headline now.

'Mayor's Daughter Caught Fucking on Family Hiking Trails.'

"I don't see anything," Gray replies, tucking himself back into his pants that will have to be dry cleaned now, at the very least. He starts the engine, rolling the windows down to combat the fog we created.

I try to dismiss the thought, but something keeps niggling there. I scan the tree line, hoping it's just my imagination running wild. A tree branch snaps and we both whirl around to look out my side of the car where a figure in all black is approaching the SUV.

"Uh, for some reason, I don't think they're looking for a ride," I glance at Gray, he doesn't look concerned.

"Can we go?" I ask while rolling my window up. My heart starts up an odd rhythm in my chest, panic tries to grip me as the figure makes their way closer.

The car lurches forward and the black clad person darts into the path of our escape. Gray honks the horn at them, but they tilt their head, like every killer from any horror movie ever made. I can't see their face, it's obscured by a black cloth, only their eyes are visible, and they look flat. Emotionless. Resigned.

"Go," I say, not caring if Gray has to run this person over.

"I can't just run them over!" Gray shouts, like he read my mind.

Something long and silver slowly drops from the masked person's black sweater sleeve. The same glint I swore I saw earlier winking in and out. I suck in a breath as realization sinks in.

They are wielding a butcher's knife.

"They have a knife! *Now* can you run them over?" I screech.

Gray honks again and edges the car closer to where the person is standing.

They don't move.

It's as if they don't believe Gray will run them over, or they don't care if they die.

Chapter Five

The person lays the tip of the large knife against the grill of the SUV, slowly dragging it back and forth. The scratching noise is loud in the silence of the night. Scary, like one of those thriller movies come to life.

"Gray, please," I murmur, as if the quieter I am, the better chance I have of the masked creep not seeing me.

He revs the engine again, slowly pushing the Mercedes against the assailant, warning them away. Quick as lightning the figure moves, dragging the knife across the hood and door of Gray's side. The masked person slams the butt of the knife into Gray's window, shattering the glass—it sounds like heavy rain on a gloomy day—one gloved hand reaching for Gray's neck.

It all happens within seconds and Gray smashes the gas to make the SUV punch forward, dragging the masked assailant along with us. They grapple for purchase on the ledge of the broken window, causing Gray to swerve around all over the lot.

I'm screaming, fumbling with my phone, trying to call 911, when the car halts to a stop right at the edge of the entrance to the hiking trails. Gray sputters, hands flying to his neck. I look over at him and see red pools in his hands, spilling over his fingers. The red rivulets I know in my bones are his blood.

He turns to look at me, his eyes wide and turning glassy.

"Run," he chokes out. Before the masked murderer rips the knife from his neck and Gray's blood sprays the inside of the cabin, as well as my face.

I pull on the handle, trying and failing to get the door to unlock. I can see the person out of the corner of my eye opening Gray's door and hauling him out. Thanking God I didn't put my seatbelt on, I finally get the door open and fall out onto the rough gravel.

The knife wielder lunges across the seat, gripping my hair in their fist. I feel my throat shred as I scream in agony while they try to lift me back into the car.

I scramble for something, anything on the ground that I can use to get their hand out of my hair. But my fingers are slippery with sweat and Gray's blood.

They swing the knife down—the woosh of it is so loud in the otherwise quiet area—cleaving my hair, and clipping my temple. It takes a moment for the pain to register, but their hand comes away with my hair as I roll onto the trail beside the parking lot.

Picking myself up, I bolt for the trees. Praying they won't follow.

My prayers go unanswered as I hear their footsteps pounding across the gravel in my direction. My heart is beating out of my chest as I push my legs to go faster than I've ever asked them to go before.

Branches reach and scratch at my exposed stomach, the flesh opening in thin splits. But I'm not concerned with that right now. I hear them crash through the trees, I'm a good distance ahead, but their strides are longer.

I have to hide.

There is no way I can outrun them.

I swing myself up on a thick branch of a low hanging tree, pausing and trying to calm my breathing so I can hear if they approach. Blood pounds in my ears, adrenaline pumps through my veins, fear and anxiety push me to look around.

The woods are silent, minus the chirping of crickets and occasional hoot of an owl. I use the exercises I learned in therapy to control my breathing. Assessing the view and keeping my ears open for the stranger in case they approach, I glance up.

My phone chimes with a voice. It's still clutched in my hand, and how I managed to hold on to it I have no idea. The 911 operator's voice comes through the speaker, and I cringe.

Can *they* hear it?

I whisper into the phone, "There's a-a person, they're d-dressed in all black, th-they have a knife." I sputter the story to her in a rush, keeping my ears perked to hear anything that could be them.

"And where are you now?" She asks, I can hear her finger nails clicking on a keyboard.

"I'm in a tree beside the entrance to the Gravity Hill trails, near Highway 72," I breathe, trying to help determine how far in, "I don't know how far into the woods I ran. They..the person..." a sob breaks through my chest, "They killed him."

"Breathe for me miss," she replies, stalling a little, "What's your name?"

"Fern."

It was her turn to suck in a breath, she knows who I am, without me having to spell it out.

I can hear it in her voice when she says, "Okay Fern, we'll get to you as soon as we can."

"Thank you," I sigh and hang up. My muscles are trying to relax against the rough bark of the tree, when underbrush snaps and crackles as the assailants boots come into view. I hold my phone over my mouth, stifling the scream that wants to roar out of my body.

They look around slowly, moving like they know I'm here somewhere. They haven't spoken. Not a word, so I listen as hard as I can, just in case I can identify them if they do speak.

I'm not high enough though, if they look up they will be able to see me. So I carefully peel myself off the thick trunk and use all my strength to quietly pull my weight up onto a higher branch, positioning myself on the opposite side of the tree from them. Adrenaline adds to my dexterity, because there is no way I could have pulled myself up this high on a normal day.

Their head swivels in the direction of my last hiding spot and I choke back another scream. Silently thanking God that I moved not two seconds ago. If I hadn't.... a shiver races up my spine thinking of the possibilities.

When the assailant stalks further into the woods, I chance a call to my brother. Manson picks up on the third ring, "Yo Ferny!"

Music pulses in the background, muffled, as if he is still at Dean's.

I almost cry in relief at his voice.

"Help me," I silently sob into the receiver. "There's a person all in black with a knife, chasing me."

"Whoa. Fern? Is this a joke?" He says, sounding annoyed, and my stomach sinks.

"It's not a fucking joke," I growl. Tears running hot trails down my face as I hear a dial tone and realize that he has already hung up.

Not believing my call. Who does he think would prank him using my phone?

He was supposed to protect me.

BUT. HE. HUNG. UP.

Sobs rack my body as the thought sinks in. I can't sit up here waiting on the killer stranger to come back, what if they find me next time?

With my brain scrambled and all the wires crossed, I dial the only other person I can think of in a time like this.

He picks up on the first ring.

"Hello?" His voice is deep, like gravel rubbing together. The music is louder now, so I know they must both still be at Dean's.

"Creed," I breathe, letting the tears continue to flow, "I need help. There's a murderer...." I get out through a muffled sob, "They have a knife, they killed Gray."

"Fern?" he says incredulously. I get it. I've never called

him, not once in my life, but then he asks, "Where are you?"

"In the woods off Highway 72. Near the entrance to the trails," I fight back another sob hoping that he will get my brother and come find me. I don't have much faith in the police, "Please hurry, I think they're going to kill me."

"Fern, don't you dare hang up this fucking phone," he barks into the device, and I wince, still wondering if the person stalking the woods can hear me. I nod, as if Creed can see me, "Fern. Do you understand?" He repeats.

"Yes," I whisper, twigs snap and leaves rustle with movement to my left. I slap my hand over my mouth to stifle my terror. Whispering through my hands I say, "Creed, they're back."

Fear grips my throat. Making the words scratchy and low. The killer walks in circles under the tree I'm camped out in, "They know I'm here."

"Stop fucking talking Fern. We're on our way. Keep me in your ear until I tell you to move. Do you understand me?"

I make a small noise of acceptance, realizing the masked person can probably hear the tenor of Creed's booming voice through my phone. I consider hanging up, but don't, the tether between Creed and me is the only feeling of safety I have at the moment.

Pain slowly filters into my consciousness, and I realize

it's been there the whole time. The adrenaline must be wearing off. My head is on fire, my stomach feels like it's been through a shredder. Blood soaks through my shirt, and the bark of the tree is ripping slits in my too thin pants.

I swipe my hand across my brow and it comes away sticky with blood and sweat. I tentatively touch the knife wound on my temple, a big mistake. The gash is much wider than I thought it was. I gingerly slide my finger along the slice, feeling fresh blood ooze around the skin and roll down my face. Pulling my hand away from my head I look down at it and note that my fingernails are almost completely torn off several of my fingers.

My pulse is dipping and I can feel my body wanting to give out. I don't know how long I've been sitting here. If I fall from this height, I might die. I'll hit a few bigger branches on my way down, and if I'm lucky the fall will kill me before the masked person can.

"Fern!" I hear Creed below on my phone. It's still in my hand, resting against my leg, but I can't find the strength to pull it up to my ear. I don't know if the psychopath with the knife is still here or not, I can't get my brain to care, or react. As I hear shouts and dogs barking, flashing lights behind my closed eyelids. It all just seems too far away, like I'm not in my body and I am hearing things underwater.

I hear whispers, little snippets of conversation. My name, crying, bright lights, buzzing in my brain. I can't feel anything anymore, their phantom words are carried away on the breeze.

All thoughts seem to escape me, and my vision goes black. Fear scraping at my insides, but I can't drudge up the sense to care.

Pain ricochets through my body.

I just want it to end.

This whole nightmare, I just need it to end.

My phone slips through my fingers, falling and cracking along the way, and I feel the rush of air as I fall along with it.

She got away
from me
Through the
green branches
of the trees
Her fear was
my beacon; her
fright my
desire
Do not run
from me, my
little fire
For I will seek
and never tire

Chapter Six

My thoughts swirl and churn as bright lights illuminate behind my closed eyes. I can feel hands, everywhere. Touching, sharp stings of pain, probing. I can't speak, can't tell them to stop.

That it hurts.

I must be dying, falling into the abyss feels like hurtling through ice. Like I'm suffering for all of my bad deeds. Fabric rips, and panic slices through my body.

The murderer in the woods, they must have found me, but I don't remember leaving the woods. I don't remember coming out of the tree. Did they knock me out? I try to flail my arms, blood still pounding through my head at the speed of lighting. I can't make out any sounds.

I'm stuck in my body, unable to hear, see, or move. Like I'm trapped inside my own mind. A torture all on it's own.

How did it get this bad?

Who would want to kill me, or Gray?

My thoughts turn hazy, did they drug me?

Oh God, this cannot be good. I can't pass out again.

If I do, who knows what could happen?

I blink, my eyelids grazing over my eyeballs like sandpaper over stone. It hurts, everything hurts. The overhead lights are bright, so bright I close my eyes again. Blinking a few times to clear the awful feelings welling up inside me.

Movement makes me still. I'm not alone, I can hear a beeping sound growing rapidly stronger. The person beside me moves, towering over me as I lay here. Wherever *here* may be.

"Dad!" I hear a familiar voice call. Memories assault my senses. One after the other. Gray and I in his car. Gray's blood coating the inside of the car. The masked person who killed him. Being in a tree, bleeding with...no.

Oh no, no, no, no, no.

Manson can't be here, he hung up on me. He didn't come.

Hands circle mine and I thrash, feeling the hard plastic on either side of me bite into my arms.

I don't want him to touch me.

He left me!

"Ferny," it sounds like he's crying, but that can't be right. He isn't crying for me. Not when he left me to fucking die.

"No!" I try shouting, but my voice is hoarse, like I haven't had water in weeks. Dry and cracked sounds leave my mouth, and when I finally open my eyes the bright room is filled with shining eyes and blue people hovering around me.

One of the people in blue argues with Dad, his face red and splotchy, as another person in blue smiles down at me and pushes something through one of the tubes connected to my skin. The room grows hazy as it all clicks.

Hospital.

I am in a hospital room. As if my brain knows it can't take any more, it shuts off and blackness swallows me whole.

Beeping machines wake me from a dreamless sleep.

Slowly, I sit up from where I have been laying on a hard bed. Eyes adjusting to the dim room. It's not like before, my heart rate doesn't rise because I know I'm safe. My body aches, and tubes run from my arms to dripping bags of fluid.

The machine beside the bed beeps in a steady rhythm. The hard plastic cage around the upper part of the bed is still lifted. The seat beside the bed is empty. Light gray vinyl upholstery covers the chair, and makes the dark wood accents stand out. The room is painted in a soft blue, the only light coming from the lamp in the corner of the room.

On the other side of the room lays a couch with a few pillows and a throw haphazardly covering the empty cushions. I need to move, but all the things connecting me to machines and drip bags have me locked into the bed.

Glancing over the plastic barrier of the bed I find buttons, one marked 'call', and a few for what I assume is the TV mounted on the wall. I hit the call button and two nurses immediately come into the room.

"Miss Hayes," one of them starts. "How are you feeling?"

"Okay," I croak out.

"I'm going to get you some fresh water while Keni here undoes your monitors," she smiles, "It's good to see you awake."

I have no idea how long I've been in between reality and death. It doesn't really matter to me anymore. Nothing does, as I watch the nurse check the IV's in my arms, "I'm going to have to pull your catheter, it's not going to be pleasant."

Nodding, I lay back down. Allowing her to do what she needs so I can finally get up and out of this uncomfortable bed. When she's done, she offers me her hand. I take it, noticing for the first time the cuts along my arms.

"They may scar," she says with a sympathetic smile that I can't return. I don't care if they scar. I didn't expect to wake up, so why would I care about scars? When I don't respond, she helps pull me up and off the bed. My feet hit the floor, covered in blue fuzzy socks with grippers on the bottom.

A cool breeze opens the back of the plain white gown someone must have put me in. She leads me to the bathroom, trailing my IV pole along after me, and offers to help me bathe. I guess laying in a hospital bed for God knows how long makes a person smell.

I decline her offer, but allow her to help me untie the strings on the back of the gown, "Try not to get your head or your IV sites wet. I'll stay right outside, if you need anything."

I nod as she turns the shower on. The bathroom isn't like any hospital bathroom I've ever seen. It's decadent in a way, white subway tile lines the walls, and glass encloses the shower instead of a cheap curtain. The fixtures are shiny, and silver as if they have just been shined. Nothing at all like I would expect.

The hot water streams over my skin, sending goose bumps all over my body. Tentatively, I touch the bandage over my temple. It's thick and gauzy, then I remember the way it felt when I touched it with my hands. They must have stitched it together, now that will scar.

I sit down on the tiles, letting the water rain down on my back as the first few tears begin to flow as memories violate my thoughts. The events of that night swarming back through my mind at a rapid pace. Manson hanging up, Creed screaming through the phone for me to stay where I was.

"Where is she?" Muffled voices flow through the wooden lacquered door of the bathroom. Assaulting my ears in a way that has fresh tears flowing faster and sobs racking my body. Wails soon leave my lips as rage and sadness cloud my every thought.

"Ferny!" I hear my brother's shout. I didn't think I could cry any harder, but now my tears mingle with the pounding of the water and swirl down the drain. Flowing out in a torrent of devastation. The knob turns and I scream. I don't know I'm doing it until my brother's face is visible through the foggy glass. Fear, pain, and anguish roar through me.

"Go away," I rage, voice cracking and breaking. He takes another step into the room and my cries turn into shrieks, as if I'm being attacked all over. I scramble into the furthest corner of the shower where the water doesn't hit, and the IV is tugged violently from my arm. I barely register the pain, or the blood.

His face twists in confusion and heartbreak. But I can't care, I *don't* care how he feels. He left me. He was my life line, and he severed that tie without a thought. A large hand lands on his shoulder, pulling him out of the bathroom. My mother walks in then, hair disheveled, worry lines marking her brow, eyes red and puffy.

"My little Fern," she cries, tears dripping down her makeup-free face. I haven't seen my mother without makeup in... well, I can't remember when. She slides to her knees outside of the glass, "I'm so sorry."

It's not her fault, I know that. Yet I can't bring myself to speak to her. To voice anything after seeing my brother. My heart twists painfully behind my ribs, torn in two. Wanting to believe he is sorry, that he regrets that moment ever since it happened.

I just... can't.

The hospital must have an unlimited supply of hot water. The spray of the shower is still hot by the time the nurses rush back in and help my mother out, while the other tries to coax me out of my corner to hold the wound on my arm closed so she can stop the bleeding.

In my haste to get as far away from Manson as I could, I also soaked the bandage in my hair, so the nurse carefully washes it for me. Once she's done, she dries me off as if I can't do it myself. I can, I just don't care too. My memories keep blurring, "how did I get here?"

It comes out a whisper, broken into pieces.

"You don't remember?" The nurse, Keni, asks while brushing out my hair before re-bandaging the stitched up wound, and my arm.

"Not much," I admit.

"I think your parents are waiting in your room," she squeezes my shoulders before making eye contact with me in the mirror, "It may be best for them to fill you in."

"Mans..."

She interrupts as if she knows what I was going to ask and shakes her head, "Big brute took him outside."

Creed.

It had to be him. He saved me, I can feel it in the very marrow of my bones.

But why is he here?

Keni leads me back into the bed, freshly clothed in sweats of my own. She says she'll be back to hook up my new IV with pain meds.

I'm not sure I need them, I feel numb enough already.

Chapter Seven

My parents hover over the bed where I sit cross legged. We stare at each other, no one is sure how to start a conversation.

Finally Dad breaks the silence, "I'm so sorry, Fern."

He barely has the words out as a single tear spills free and trails down his cheek.

"What happened?" I ask, unsure where they will start.

They look at each other before a police officer waltzes into the room accompanied by a well dressed man in a brown suit. On anyone else it would look ridiculous, but on this man it looks well tailored. His rich dark skin is unblemished, and the watch on his wrist tells me he makes far more money than a regular detective.

"I'm detective Kimp," he says by way of greeting. His smile is small and guarded, "I was hoping you could fill us in on the events of your attack."

"She just woke up for God's sake!" My mother cries.

"How long have I been out?" I ask no one in particular.

"Two days," Detective Kimp informs me. As if that might make me feel better. If a detective is here that means they don't have a clue where the person who attacked me—and killed Gray—is.

"You haven't caught him, have you?"

His eyes narrow, "Him?"

"The man who killed Gray." I swallow, "The man who chased me into the woods."

"You sound sure it was a male. Did you see his face?"

"It was covered."

"So it could have been anyone?"

"No, he was strong, strong enough to hold himself up while the car was still moving to kill Gray," I eye my father.

He didn't know Gray and I were casually sleeping together, I didn't want the man to get fired. Although, now it doesn't matter, does it? He's gone and it's my fault.

"Can you walk me through the events of that night?" The detective asks, eyeing the uniformed officer near the door and subtly motioning for them to wait outside, "no detail is too small."

I glance toward my parents, I'm not embarrassed about my behavior. I am a woman with no limits. Experimenting is something people do. But they look worse for wear, and two days of constant worry about your youngest child's survival takes its toll.

"Go home, I'll be fine," truthfully, I just don't want to be around anyone right now. I don't want to talk to this detective. However, he doesn't look like the type to give up easily.

"No, Fern," my father starts, "we're staying."

I shake my head, willing them to leave.

"I'm fine. Promise," I am not, in fact, fine. But they don't put up a fight as Keni comes back in with packages and another bag of liquid to hook me up to. They both kiss the part of my forehead that isn't currently covered in bandages before walking out the door. Leaving Keni, the detective and me, alone with the cop outside of the door.

After relaying my side of the story, Detective Kimp pauses writing in his notebook, "Why did you disconnect the 911 call?"

"I wanted to call my brother. Because I thought..." my voice doesn't want to work. I can't say it out loud. That my brother chose something else over me. I push it out anyway. Running from the truth only postpones the inevitable crash and burn. "Because I thought he would find me first."

"But he didn't, the call only lasted about four seconds once connected." The detective's eyes search my face, looking for something?

I nod.

"When you were found, your cell phone was connected to an unknown number. One that wasn't saved in your phone. Who did you call?"

It's true, I hadn't saved Creed's number. I memorized it from Manson's phone. Just in case I ever got the nerve to do something about my feelings. I *wish* that's why I'd used the number.

But how do they not know the number was Creed's?

"I can't remember," I lie.

Maybe I'm lying because I'm embarrassed. Maybe I'm lying because he isn't the person who was supposed to save me. Mostly, I'm lying because even though Manson destroyed whatever faith in him I had, I can't bring myself to bury that knife into his back.

That it was his best friend that saved me after he decided I wasn't worth his time.

My brother doesn't deserve any slack from Creed, and I won't be the person that ends another relationship.

Chapter Eight

The next day when my parents come back to the hospital, I learn about the private wing reserved just for our family. The two nurses in my room are the only ones here, and once I leave they will go back to the emergency room where they are normally stationed.

"Are you ready to come home?" My father asks.

Home.

The word sends shivers down my spine, Manson will be there. I'm not ready to see him. I can't see him. My breathing speeds up in rapid pants, "I can't." I get out between ragged breaths.

"Honey," my mother starts, "Manson would never hurt you."

But he did, he hurt me in a way that isn't visible. Where the wound doesn't fester in yellowing puss, but in growing disdain and fervor. Where the blood isn't a river running red, but a steady trickle to be collected anytime I see him

In the end, I allow them to help me into their SUV, sandwiched between the two of them like a child again. Both of them not touching or speaking to me, but about me. I zone out, I don't care what they have to say.

The gates of our house are closed, only opening when the SUV gets close enough to trigger the sensor to glide open. The house looms large, as it always has. Though none of the happiness I used to feel washes over me seeing it. Instead there's nothing, other than the dread at possibly seeing my brother.

Our security head, Jax, walks out of the house and opens the car door on my mothers side to allow us out. He gives a small smile to me before returning to his stoic expression.

I walk straight up the staircase to my room, not pausing at the obnoxiously large table filled with flowers in the foyer, and shut the door. Locking it for peace. I would have never locked it before. But I can't bring myself to unlock it. I stare at the lock, trying to feel something other than fear at what may be on the other side of the door.

I crumble into the floor, knees sinking into the plush cream carpet and cry. I can't be here. In the same house where I feel so betrayed. It isn't fair of me, because it isn't Manson's fault I was attacked. I don't *want* to hate him. I don't *want* to hate my parents for not being upset with him.

I don't want to feel anything.

I lay there, long enough for the sun to set and my room to go from bright with sun, to fuzzy with dark.

Tears long dried up, I get up and walk into my bathroom, opening the cabinets and emptying them in search of something that will make me forget.

I don't want to think of Gray, and the way he told me to run. The last word he uttered was a plea for me to get away. To save myself because he knew he was going to die. The knife as it slid out of his neck and the sound it made. The suction of his muscles and tendons trying and failing to stick to the metallic blade.

I find a bottle of pain meds the nurse told me I can take for any discomfort. My parents must've put them in here before I got home. I take four, without looking at the instructions.

I just want it to stop.

I drink water from the tap to ease them down. Curling up on the bathroom rug, and trying to think of happy memories. Anything that doesn't involve blood and knives.

Sleep finds me easily. My eyes feel heavy with it, and I don't fight it as I let myself drift away.

I wish the screaming would stop, and the jumbled words would cease. Why can't I get my mind to shut off? Why must it remind me of blood and knives?

Hands wrap around my shoulders.

Did *they* find me?

Will they finally kill me now?

"Ferny?" Shaking. So much shaking, "Ferny, please wake up."

The sound of a voice stings my ears, making me want to crawl back into the dreamless sleep I was having. Instead I'm thrust back into the nightmares constantly plaguing my consciousness. More wails pierce the air as my body leaves the tile floor of my bathroom. Wrapped in strong arms that I don't immediately recognize, but feel familiar.

Manson's voice flows over me, "I'm sorry, Ferny. I'm so fucking sorry."

TWO

YEARS

LATER

Chapter Nine

"How's Daisy treatin' you today?"

I turn, finding Noah standing in the stall doorway. I have spent over two years on this ranch and I still haven't gotten used to the look of him.

His tanned skin from hours working in the sun matches mine. Calluses cover his hands from countless ropes and leads. His striking gray eyes stand out against the slight wrinkles that dot his face.

If it weren't for him, and his mom, I don't think I would have survived past my twenty-sixth birthday.

Not after that night.

"Stubborn, as usual," I say, still running my hands over her mane. Daisy came to the horse rescue around the one year mark of my stay. I like to joke with Noah that she was my birthday present.

After Manson found me in my bathroom unresponsive, my parents shipped me off here. To rehabilitate away from the trauma of that night.

They never came back.

I'm not too upset with them. Honestly, they thought I tried to kill myself, who wants to face their child after that?

It took me over three months to venture outside of the large farmhouse to the barn. It wasn't a long walk, but I didn't have much to live for at that point. Even though Noah and Miss Loretta tried every single day to get me out of the house, I just couldn't bring myself to do it.

After the fourth month went by Miss Loretta finally told me if I didn't start doing something, anything, that she would be forced to send me to the local psych ward. That I had to want to help myself before she could do any of the hand holding she knew I needed.

I owe them everything.

These days Noah and I are as close as a doctor and patient can be. We go into town and stock up on things the house needs as well as the farm. My panic attacks have gotten so much better that they're few and far between.

"She'll go when she's ready," Noah says, ever the voice of reason. "Give her time."

"Ugh!"

Noah laughs as he offers me his hand. It's easy to reach back out and grab it as he helps haul me to my feet, and swipes the hay off my jeans. Daisy came to us pregnant, the owners had planned to breed her with a show horse champion, but she ended up getting herself into trouble before they could.

So they dropped her off here, discarded, alone, just like me. Except I wasn't pregnant, thank God.

"I can't wait! It feels like she's been pregnant forever!"

He laughs as we walk toward the barn doors, "Patience, young one."

I lightly smack his arm and laugh with him. Ever since my family dropped me off here at Rolling Oaks I've gotten my life back. Noah and Miss Loretta gave me that. They hadn't had any other people come through though, which makes me sad, and a little worried that my family might have something to do with it.

The farm doesn't seem like it's in trouble, so I never questioned anything until a few days ago when I overheard Noah on the phone with someone. He was arguing that now wasn't the time. But anytime I brought it up he just smiled and told me not to worry about it.

"So," he chirps as we make our way up to the house, "You think you'd be willin' to visit your hometown soon?"

I stop and stare at his back in shock. Not once have we talked about me going back. Or what my life would look like if I did.

I can't go back to nothing.

I can't be idle, and I know I'm no longer the party girl I was back then. He doesn't turn around, just keeps walking as if he didn't just throw cold water on my psyche.

Noah isn't only my therapist, he's also my closest friend here. So this, coming from him after everything I've accomplished, feels like it should be a step in the right direction.

Instead it feels suffocating.

My feet pick back up and follow him to the porch where he sits beside Miss Loretta, who also looks like she's ready to have a tough conversation.

"You're sending me back," I say, sinking into the opposite rocking chair. The same rocking chair where I've spilled all my dirty secrets and fears to Noah. "What did I do wrong?"

Miss Loretta, with her wrinkled hands, leans forward and clasps my hands in hers, her bony fingers squeezing mine.

"You haven't done anythin' wrong."

"You've done so well here, that I think it's time for a visit," Noah starts.

"You don't have to stay, and Noah will be with you the whole time," she tells me, allowing me to absorb what they are really saying. "Plus, you could be putting that PhD to use somewhere."

She winks at me, I know she enjoys the stories I spin for her when she's not feeling well, or having an off day. But they're just that, stories, fiction.

I have had no contact with my family since they sent me here.

"Your brother misses you. So much." Miss Loretta says quietly.

My eyes snap to hers. I've worked through the feelings I had about Manson, and while I still don't know if I'll ever trust him again, I know I forgive him.

But saying the words to him? Feels like he's getting off easy. And I know if Noah knew what I was thinking he would tell me that forgiveness is for me. Not him.

"Can I think about it?" I ask them, my eyes bouncing between the two of them.

"Of course, sweet child," Miss Loretta releases my hands and I nod, excusing myself from the conversation.

Making my way through the farmhouse and toward the room that's been mine for over two years. Its bright yellow walls feel like my safety net.

Like home.

I don't want to leave, but a part of me knows that I was always going to have to go back. That's what this place is for.

I pull out the journal I've been using since our first therapy session and flip through the pages and pages of thoughts I've had and I allow myself the space to just feel. To analyze my thoughts and place them where they need to go.

Writing on the first blank page, I scribble my notions...

Chapter Ten

Noah loads our bags into the SUV my parents sent to pick us up. Shutting the hatch, Miss Loretta gives me one final squeeze, before I slide into the leather covered seats. Noah grips my hand as the driver takes off slowly down the gravel drive.

"It's just a visit," Noah squeezes reassuringly.

I wish I could believe him, but so many things about home must have changed. It's been two years for fucks sake, and I'm almost twenty-eight. Things have certainly changed for me.

I end up watching the valleys and grassy hills fly by as we make our way toward the town where I used to buy fresh flowers for the vase Miss Loretta bought me. Where I would wait on Noah to finish his coffee with friends and write in my journal.

The memories surface, until sleep finally pulls me under.

"Fern." Noah's voice is rough with sleep as he lightly

shakes my shoulder, "We're here."

My eyes flutter open and the same house I grew up in stands tall before me. As if nothing has changed. As if I am the same carefree person I was before my whole life imploded. But I'm not the same girl who partied and lived without a care in the world.

Not even close.

The old brick house looks impossibly bigger than it did before. The white pillars look freshly cleaned, and the front porch is minimally decorated. A big contrast to how it used to look. My mother never used to spare a penny on decorations.

He finds my hand again, anchoring me in the moment. It's been nearly two years since that night, and nothing like it has plagued Gravity Hill since then. Noah made sure to keep up with the case, until it went cold and they closed it.

That sent me into another spiral; knowing Gray would have no justice for his murder.

I didn't love him, but he was a gentle man, who always made sure I was taken care of and safe.

He didn't deserve what happened.

My mother opens the heavy wooden door as Noah holds tightly to my hand while I get out of the car. Her eyes are already red with tears, and I notice she has gained some weight since I saw her last. Which, if you knew my mother, you would know that her weight is something she rigorously maintains.

It feels odd seeing her without my father, they used to be a pair that always went together no matter what they were doing. Candy appears next, no one saying anything, and no one taking a step to breach the divide of the driveway.

Candy's hands go up to her mouth as tears fall from her eyes. She looks older somehow, as if she too has aged beyond the two years since I last saw her. Her hair is cut at her shoulders in a severe bob with blonde streaks that add dimension to her dark hair. She feels familiar, but completely divergent from the Candy I remember.

I know logically that life moved on for her. That she hasn't been waiting around for me to get better and come back, but it feels...off, like there is something missing.

Then my father appears and wastes no time coming to me and wrapping me up in his arms. I immediately stiffen at the affection.

His hug isn't like Miss Loretta's. Where she's frail and loving, my father is strong and sobers a part of me I have been scared of. Lifting my arms, I hug him back, breathing in his aftershave.

"I told your mother to wait, and now look at me," he laughs

through a thick throat. His eyes have gone softer, his beard a bit more gray.

"It's okay," I say, and I find that I actually mean it. As I reach back for Noah's hand, Manson comes out of the house. He's larger now, at thirty three, his body has filled out from what I assume is time spent in the gym. He never really cared about things like that before, but maybe it was his form of therapy. I had Noah and the ranch, what did my brother have?

Still lean through the midsection but larger in the chest and arms. His face is a plethora of emotions. When my eyes finally land on his, my breath flies from my lungs.

Creed is standing just behind him. Still inside the house, but my eyes find him nonetheless. His green eyes are trained on me, burning a hole through my chest as Candy moves to be beside Manson. Creed has always been the bigger of the two, but now he's a mountain of a man. His beard is thick and neatly trimmed. His long dirty blonde hair pulled behind his head in a knot, shaved just above the ears.

My knees want to give out.

I want to melt into the gravel under his stare. I've been away too long to still have this kind of reaction to a man I've never touched.

But logic rarely makes an appearance where my heart is concerned.

Noah clears his throat and I tear my eyes away from Creed to look at him. He nods toward my brother and drops hold of my hand to shake Mansons.

When I look up again, my parents, and Creed are gone. It's just Noah, me, and Manson. He opens his arms and I take a tentative step forward. When I'm close enough, he wraps his arms around me. His shoulders are shaking, and he sinks to the ground, taking me with him. Our knees touch as he hugs me.

"I'm sorry," he keeps whispering over and over again.

I let him hold on to me, until the sharp rocks bite into my skin and he is no longer sobbing. I give him a small smile when we lean apart, "I know it wasn't your fault."

Relief crosses his face and he wipes his eyes, "I've missed you so much."

Noah steps up beside us and offers his hand. I take it as Manson gets up and helps carry our stuff inside.

It's all so much, like a blur of motion as you cluck your horse to a run. My breath gets stuck in my lungs as we cross the threshold of the house I didn't expect to return to. I can feel my muscles locking up, refusing to move even an inch more into the house.

I don't see anyone as Noah places a reassuring hand on my lower back and whispers, "You are safe, Fern."

His hand falls away and he stands there, waiting for me to make the decision to stay or leave. After I take a few deep breaths I nod to him and together we ascend the stairs to the room I almost don't recognize.

Everything looks the same, but the feeling of home isn't there anymore. I don't feel anything. Not sadness, or anger, just...nothing.

Noah puts our bags on the bed and sits, patting the mattress beside him in invitation. I cross the room. Leaving the door open, I have gotten so used to it at the farm, it's basically second nature. But the hallway doesn't lead to a little couch and four walls and a cozy kitchen that only produces home cooked meals.

"What are you feeling?" Noah asks.

"I don't know," I shrug, "Nothing?"

I'm not sure of anything anymore, being in this house has warped my sense of reality. Nothing is wrong, or out of place, except me. It's like my parents created a time capsule for me, but I don't belong here, I'm no longer that woman.

He gives me a look that clearly says he doesn't believe me. Maybe I'm not allowing myself to feel. I'm not relieved to be home, I'm not anxious, it's just that so many thoughts are swirling in my mind, I don't know which one to analyze first.

"Everything," I finally tell him.

Seeing Creed was the first thing that had my heart beating double in my chest, but I felt safe. Except now he's gone, along with everyone else, presumably to give me space to settle.

"I'll leave you to get settled and go over your calmin' strategies with your parents before dinner," he leans over and bumps my shoulder with his, "Okay?"

I nod and watch him walk away.

The curtains are open, and I stare at the view below which is exactly the same as I remember. The trees that ring the property are still tall and beautiful.

The only thing that feels different...is me.

Chapter Eleven

A knock breaks my concentration on the trees. A shadow moves over the door and once the view is clear in the window and I see it's Candy, my shoulders relax.

I turn, facing her fully. She's different too, her long legs are covered in denim, and her blouse is one button shy of promiscuous. If we went back in time, those buttons would never have been closed.

Her eyes are watery as she takes me in.

"Hi," she says, her voice cracking with the unshed tears she's holding back.

"You can cry," I tilt my head, still looking her over for the differences in her, "It's okay."

Her tears run freely as she makes her way toward me. She reaches out and I instinctively step back. My shoulders hit the glass panes and my feet slip on the soft carpet. Hurt flashes across her features, as if she expected something different.

I'm not scared of her, I just don't want to touch anyone right now. With all of my senses taking in everything, I just...can't take on her emotions too. I'm already overstimulated.

"I'm sorry," she says, as she drops her arms.

"You don't have anything to be sorry for," I reply, even though my voice feels different in this place that I once felt invincible.

"I didn't stop you from leaving that night, I..." she trails off as Manson makes his way into the room. His hand covers Candy's back as he stares at me. Probably looking for my differences too.

His eyes trail from my hair down to my boots. I don't think he's ever seen me in anything remotely close to work gear, so his eyebrows raise slightly, "Noah seems nice."

I nod, because he is. In his line of work it helps.

"You look great, Ferny," he says, reaching out a hand. I look at it, wondering what exactly he wants me to do. Does he want me to make the first step in reclaiming our friendship? Or does he simply want to touch me to make sure I'm here? To make sure I'm real.

When I don't take his hand, he laces his fingers with Candy's, "Dinner is in a few. Do you want to head down with us?"

I zero in on their hands, and emotions start to fester as I connect the dots. I try not to rush to conclusions as Noah would want me to ask before assuming. My heart flutters at the possibility that they finally got their shit together. It's a bit odd, feeling something other than… nothing.

Footsteps pull me from my thoughts as my mother appears, "Dinner is ready. Fern, baby, are you joining us?"

I'm not sure if I should. It was a long ride here and I've done well since returning. I don't want to spiral and sacrifice my progress. But my stomach rumbles, making the decision for me.

"Sure," I answer, following behind Candy and Manson as they lead the way, their hands still linked.

The house is just like it was when I left, spotless and tidy. But the staff all have unfamiliar faces, it unnerves me a bit to wonder what happened to the old staff. Did they quit, or simply leave?

Empty plates are waiting, with silverware and napkins placed at each chair. Mom and Dad sit at the opposite ends of the table, while the rest of us file in. I sit next to my father, like I always have and Manson takes the seat on his other side, across from me. I wonder if they left my seat empty all this time.

Waiting, and hoping, for their energetic daughter to

return.

Candy slips into the seat beside Manson and Noah sits across from her, on the other side of me. His small smile of encouragement sits between us in the silence. The cook unveils a few platters boasting rosemary chicken, stuffed peppers, baked broccoli, and sweet potato pie. The smell is divine, and my mouth starts to water.

Since when do my parents eat southern country food? Maybe they did it for me? We each serve ourselves, serving ware clatters on the china as the silence builds. No one knows what to say, and it's weird. I know they want to ask about how I'm feeling, how I'm settling, because they hope that I'll stay.

They *want* me to stay.

I know it by the way my mother's smile is teary and the way my father's hand slowly gets closer to mine. They want me safe, and loved. I know Noah told them it would be a lot harder for me to get back into my old way of life, if I ever did.

"So, Noah, how long have you been a psychiatrist?" My brother asks.

Noah wipes his mouth after swallowing the bite he just shoved into his mouth, "About ten years now."

"I'd love to ask you a few things. Growing my client list

has taken a bit longer than I anticipated," Manson tells him. I almost forgot that my brother was also a psychiatrist, and that he's had his own practice for two years.

"Sure, anything to help a fellow doctor out." Noah looks to me, "If that's okay with Fern."

"I don't care," I shrug, because I honestly don't. I don't have an opinion either way. None of this matters to me. Gray's killer, and my would-be killer, is still out there.

Noah drinks from the wine glass that was poured, his cheeks flushing pink from the alcohol and Manson thanks him.

"Been a few years now, you have any patients?" I ask, because it feels like something a sister would ask. Making conversation.

Manson's surprise is evident, he didn't expect me to ask. He clears his throat, "Uhm, yeah. I have a few."

Candy stops eating, her eyes trained on Manson, and I can't take the subtle looks anymore. "Are you two fucking, or something?"

"Fern!" My mother bellows, and my father hides a laugh behind his napkin.

"What?" I ask, "it's a valid question."

Manson and Candy both look between me and each other, then Candy wraps her hand around Manson's and says the two words I never thought I'd hear, "We're married."

The food on my tongue goes sour, and I spit it out on my plate so I don't choke, "I'm sorry, what?" I ask, still unsure that I heard her correctly.

"We didn't know how to tell you..." Manson starts, but I hold up a hand to stop him.

"You mean to tell me you married my best friend and didn't even send me an *invitation*?" I ask, still unwilling to believe it. "When?"

"We've been married for a little over a year and a half," Manson says proudly, as if he didn't just break my heart... again.

"Over a year and a half?" I ask, to be sure. Because if that's the case, they didn't wait long after my attack. Which means....

"I'm going to ask you this one time," I say, my voice even, but gravely, "Were you two together when I called you that night?"

I'm glad they found happiness, I basically pushed them together, but at what cost? Noah covers my hand on the table. The one currently holding a knife, "I don't think that's a good road to travel down, Fern." He slips the cold metal from my fingers as I wait for one of them to answer me, "Not tonight."

"We had no idea—"

I thrust my chair backward, standing up and slamming my hands on the table, palm and fingers splayed out beside my almost untouched plate. "I nearly *died* that night," I whisper as tears roll down my cheeks, and my heart breaks all over again knowing my brother blew me off because he was busy with my best friend. "Gray did die!"

Fire burns through my veins, and my body vibrates.

Manson's eyes turn red as he stands, sending his chair into the wall in his fervor to get to me. I throw my hands up in front of my body, shielding myself from his attempt at comfort.

His face falls.

"So fucking my best friend was the thing that really kept you from coming to help me," I spit.

"That's not fair, Fern."

"*That's not fair?*" I wail and throw his words back at him, "Was Gray's death fair? Was losing my mind with fear fair? Was scrambling up a tree to avoid being killed, fair?!"

"I was high, out of my mind..." He looks genuinely remorseful, but I don't have it in me to care right now.

My chest is heaving as I walk to the door. I pause to look back, to watch the emotions flit across their faces.

"Life's not fair," I say, directing that at Candy. Because if she knew I called, and that he hung up, it makes her just as guilty.

I don't want to hear their excuses, I don't want to hear their cries. So I walk out to the back patio, where the furniture is covered in bright blue cushions and the stars are out.

Letting loose a guttural shriek from deep in my chest, I close my eyes. Tears spill through my lashes, as I sob. The pit of emotions I hadn't been prepared to handle, floor me.

I wish I could go back to not feeling.

To being numb.

But I can't. I've been sober for a year, completely off painkillers and alcohol. The regulated medicine Noah has prescribed is the only drug I put in my system now. I refuse to sink back into that black hole.

Just as I sit and cradle my head in my hands to try and gain control of myself, I hear something. Rustling stirs in the trees a few feet away, but it's too late for birds to be out, and the bugs all seem to be content croaking their tunes.

A jolt of fear runs up my spine as the noise sounds again.

Chapter Twelve

There's movement out of the corner of my eye, a dark shadow that moved only an inch. Working on the farm made my senses more... alert.

I jump up and turn to pull the door open, terror gripping my stomach as I get inside and turn the lock. Looking out the window the shadow is gone, there's nothing there.

My muscles relax as I take a step back, straight into something solid.

Everything in my body is telling me that I should run, because there shouldn't be anything there. Taking off through the house, scrambling in my boots to find purchase before I hit the stairs.

My boots hit the steps with a loud clack, chairs scrape the floors as my family runs from the dining room to see what's going on.

"Fern!" I hear a familiar voice bellow. I stop mid step, my boots going quiet.

I turn, in time to see Creed standing at the bottom of the stairs and my family rushing through the hall, Noah leading the charge. He passes Creed on his way to me, his hands brush over my shoulders as he speaks, but I can't hear him. I don't know what he's saying. All I can hear is the pounding of my heart as I drink Creed in.

The swell of his shoulders, his hand gripping the banister. The way the dress shirt he's wearing is tailored perfectly to him. How he looks impossibly bigger than he did before.

"Fern, look at me," Noah says as he pinches my chin between his fingers. I let him lead my head so our eyes latch, "What happened?"

"I saw something in the yard." I tell him, shaking my head. Noah's hand falls away, "It was nothing. Sorry."

Noah looks at me like he doesn't believe me, but lets me walk up the rest of the stairs to my old room. He trails in behind me, and shuts the door.

"Lock it," I demand.

"Fern," Noah starts, as if he can change my mind, or talk me through another illusion my mind may have conjured up, "I know it's a lot being back-"

"No, you don't. You *think* you know because of your fancy degrees and your years hearing the stories, but you really don't *know*," I whirl, "Lock. That. Door."

He does as I ask without any more words. Closing us in this room feels like the safest course of action right now.

I strip, uncaring if he's looking. He's seen it before when I've had an episode in the shower. I feel nothing for Noah in the way of intimacy, and he has only ever been professional toward me in return. He's always had that boundary between us, and I've respected it.

Because I haven't wanted to get close enough to anyone for intimate reasons since that night.

I don't think I can.

Gathering my sleep shorts and t-shirt, I head into the adjoining bathroom. The glass shower starts when I press a button on the wall, steam starts to billow through the room as I place my clothes on the counter and steady my breathing.

Thoughts spiral through my head.

The shadow, Manson and Candy. Then there's Creed, everything in my body wants to settle on him, just as it always did growing up. It was always Creed. Although, I don't know if he's the same Creed I knew. Everyone seems to have moved on and lived in the time I've been gone, and I know it's selfish to think, but how *could* they when I wasn't here?

I don't think my heart can take it if Creed's married, or

seeing someone.

I shouldn't have agreed to come here. Noah thought it would be beneficial, but so far it's caused more heartache than closure.

The water scalds my skin as I step into the shower, it feels good to sense something other than anger and fear. I let the water flow over me, turning my skin pink.

New bottles of my body wash and hair care line the shelves along the shower and it makes me want to cry. It's like they expected me to be the other version of me, the one they remember. But that was before I watched someone I cared about be butchered like a deer, and then run for my life as I was hunted for sport. Before my memories got hazy so I don't fully remember what happened to me.

I lather my hair and rinse, letting the water run through the strands. I wash my body next, scrubbing until it's raw and tender. As if I can scrub my thoughts away.

The water stops when I open the glass door, a feature I missed while I was away. I towel off and dress quickly, wrapping my hair up into a towel, before brushing my teeth.

Something catches my eye as I bend down to spit into the sink.

It looks like paper wedged between the wall and the toilet lid. Dread fills my stomach, and my skin prickles all over.

"Noah?" I ask.

He doesn't answer, so I assume he left, or fell asleep.

Slowly I tiptoe over to the toilet, and bend down to look closer. Wedging my nail against the wall and my thumb against the other side I pluck the paper from where it was hiding. It's folded neatly with crisp edges. As if the sender ran their nail over each fold before placing it here.

The paper seems oddly thick, too heavy for notebook paper.

My curiosity gets the best of me and I slowly unfold the square. It crinkles as if it's been here a while and the paper has gotten moist and dried a few times. Sticking to its edges I have to pry it open.

Something falls out, but I can't seem to focus on it. Scribbled writing fills the page, harsh red lines that I can't make sense of. I twist the paper a few times to view it at different angles.

There, an image is carved into the lines, darker than the rest. It's a woman, and a horse.

Then I notice the odd shading of the horse, and the length of the woman's hair.

It's me, right before we came back here. I cut off a lot of my hair, but the length of it in the picture, and the way she's standing, it is clearly me. I drop the paper and cover my mouth.

Thinking this has to be something Noah did, he probably drew it and didn't want me to know. The paper lands on the wrong side, beside what looks like a piece of a puzzle.

Everything I have been holding inside barrels out of me. My eyes dart around the room. This had to be some cruel joke. The person who killed Gray can't still be looking for me.

Shouts and echoes begin at my door. Banging and splintering reverberate through the space on the other side of my bathroom. I can't make my feet move, it feels as if they are rooted to the floor.

Creed busts the door down, wood flies in all directions, shattering glass and landing on my feet. His face is stone, eyes sweeping over my body. They land on the paper still laying on the floor.

He crosses the room, boots crunching on the parts of the door that splintered off, and grinding the glass underneath.

Picking up the paper he scans it. I've known Creed since I was little, so when he finally finds the image through all the scribbles his eyes darken and his fist crinkles the paper.

"What is this?" he growls, picking up the puzzle piece and turning it over to read the inscription.

"It's me."

She, thinks
she's been
alone
In the comfort
of her pretend
home
I'll show her
right from
wrong
In my arms
where she
belongs

Chapter Thirteen

I can't sleep. Especially after the chaos that ensued when Creed saw the items I found left in my bathroom.

I also can't leave my room. I don't want to risk running into my brother, or my...sister-in-law. The shadows of the house are scarier than I remember. Even in my room, the shadows seem bigger, growing as I stare at them.

Throwing my legs over the side of the bed I pull open the heavy velvet curtains. The moon is high and full, bathing the room in soft bluish light. I can see every corner now, but instead I look outside.

The tall full trees rustle and move. I imagine the small animals that jump between their limbs, happy and content in their normal life. Abruptly, I'm reminded of bleeding and clinging to bark, praying I wouldn't be spotted. Shaking my head of the memories, I stare at the bed and wonder if I should try to sleep, but I'm too restless.

Instead I rummage through the boxes in my closet. Filled

with memories and photographs, ribbons and trophies.

These things don't feel like me anymore. As if the person I was is no longer inside of me.

I stall on a picture of Manson and Creed. They have their arms around me, I'm smiling at the camera. Manson is smiling too, his signature smirk before ruffling my hair. But Creed isn't looking at the camera. His smile is wide, even though his face is turned, I can see his eyes are on me.

It was my eighteenth birthday and Manson was finally taking me out to one of his college parties. I remember Creed and him arguing about my clothes with me, they demanded that I change, but mom told them to quit pestering me about it so we could get to the party.

Candy was also invited, but we had to pick her up. So she wasn't in the picture. It was just the three of us playing dress up. Kids thinking they were adults.

Yawning, I close the boxes after packing them back up. Everything except for the picture, I slide that under all of the things in my nightstand.

I need to sleep because I'm sure that Noah has plans for me tomorrow. To test my ability to function in society. It was his whole purpose for making me come back here.

Harsh sunlight pulls me from my dreamless sleep. Right before there is a knock on the door. My room looks the same as it did when I left.

When I couldn't take it anymore and felt like the only solution was to swallow a few of the pills the doctor prescribed me and sleep. Blissful, quiet sleep with no nightmares, or terrors. I didn't read the bottle, and my family suffered for it.

I was blue and unresponsive. It wasn't a call for help, it was an accident. I assumed my parents found me, who else would be in my room after the hospital finally released me in the early morning hours? My parents shipped me off after that, so quickly I hadn't even come out of my stupor until a few days later, at the farm and hooked up to fluids.

That's when I learned Manson was actually the one who found me, unresponsive.

Noah introduced himself and why I was at the farm, he asked me about anything I remembered. Except I didn't remember much, the only night that played on repeat in my head over and over and over was...

The night I tried to forget.

"Fern," Creed's deep voice filters through the door, "If you don't answer, I'll bust the door down."

"I'm fine," I say, and I am. Or at least I think I am.

"Get dressed," he bellows.

Feelings surface that I thought had long since died. I want to stick my tongue out at the door, as if he can see me.

Surprise shocks my system, I haven't had an inkling of playfulness since that night and it feels strange. Part of me keeps thinking I don't deserve to live and be happy, the other part knows that isn't what Gray would have wanted.

I know, in my heart of hearts, that he would want me to be living. Experiencing life as I was always meant to, but with this puzzle piece and drawing fresh on my mind, it's as if I'm being pulled back into that night.

Taking a deep breath I slide out of bed, enjoying the warm carpet instead of the cool hardwood floors at the ranch. Padding over to the closet I eye my old wardrobe. None of the clothes in here will fit.

I've lost a bit of weight working on the farm. Sure I still have my curves and stretch marks, but the labor from the farm has toned up my body. My stomach is still curved over my waist, just a bit smaller, so I rummage through the bags I packed from the ranch. Pulling out my favorite pair of worn jeans, and sliding each leg into the holes and tugging them up.

I throw on a plain bra and t-shirt to complete the outfit. I don't care that it isn't designer, or that if we go into town, people will most definitely stare. I'm comfortable, like the outfit was a shield.

My shoes however, I was happy to see, had been untouched. Other than the cleaners making sure they were pristine and dust free. Heels, flats, wedges, all of them were here, and now I can add my boots to the collection, though they will need to be cleaned.

Horse shit isn't exactly the vibe I'm going for.

Pulling on my favorite pair of sneakers and lacing them up, I stand, glancing in the mirror at the version of me I have grown accustomed to. I've changed, my hair is now cut shorter, right at my shoulder blades, and lighter than it has ever been, being in the sun day in and day out. My waist is trimmer, but still solid, it will take more than farm work for me to see abs.

I feel beautiful.

Not vapidly so, but because I haven't been wearing makeup and freckles have popped up over the bridge of my nose and cheeks, I no longer feel the need to constantly wear it like armor.

Taking time to breathe and center myself, I cross the room to my nightstand where I hadn't noticed a new cell phone until now. It's shiny and as I stare at it, I'm unsure if I want to pick it up.

Not having one felt freeing, and it's been a while since I've even thought of using one.

The knob of my door wiggles, followed by a knock.

"Fern," Noah's voice comes from the other side.

Going to the door, I decide to leave the phone, it will be here when I get back, and I'm not quite ready for it yet.

"Hey," I greet him as I pull the door open.

"You ready for today?"

I nod and give him a small smile. I don't know what the plan is, but as Noah and I descend the stairs, I find everyone in the living room, spread throughout. All eyes turn to us and I pause.

My pulse starts to rise with all the attention on me.

"We had a whole day planned," my father starts, "But with last night, we weren't sure if you'd be willing to venture out."

I smile, he means it's okay to take baby steps, and I run to him. He was never a soft man, but the way he is giving me options feels like a huge milestone. I wrap my arms around his middle and breathe in his spicy scent.

His arms immediately wind around my shoulders and he

shudders. When I pull back I find his eyes glassy and his smile wide.

"Thank you," I whisper.

He nods and releases me, and when I turn around I lock eyes with Candy. Her facial expression looks sad, but I am nowhere near ready to burden myself with working through my emotions about her and my brother yet.

I'm saving that for my journal tonight.

"We have brunch reservations at Café Le Rouge," my mother says sniffling.

"My favorite."

We pile into two cars. Candy, Manson, and Creed in the smaller one in front of the SUV Noah and I arrived in. Mom and Dad join Noah and I, with me sandwiched between my mother and Noah in the back seat, and dad in the front with the driver.

"Why is he here?" I ask no one in particular.

"Creed?" My father says.

"Yeah."

"Honey, he's always around," my mother says, side eyeing me.

"Why today?" I ask.

My father turns in his seat, giving me a small smile, "We had to make a few changes after the..." he trails off, clearly trying to put together his words, "Accident."

"Changes?"

Noah lays a hand over mine, squeezing. I whip my head to look at him, but his stare remains firmly locked outside the window.

Chapter Fourteen

"You fucking *bastard*!" I launch myself out of the SUV once Noah gets out, and head straight for Creed. I am furious, and his lips are curling into a smile.

"Hello, wife," he says, loud enough Manson sinks into his shoulders.

They all knew. I had been married off while I was in the hospital. The fucking hospital, healing and going insane with fear and guilt, and my parents sold me off.

"How dare you," I spit, placing my hands on his chest and pushing as hard as I can. I'm fuming, and seeing red.

"Fern," Noah cautions, reaching for me.

"Don't lay another hand on her if you want to keep them attached to your body," Creed growls.

I hit him again, to no avail. He's fucking massive, towering over me, "You don't get to make those demands!"

He grips my wrists, and it feels like a streak of lighting hits me. I freeze instantly, my lungs seize, and my brain short circuits.

"Oh, but I do," he croons once he's leaned down close enough that his breath ghosts over my ear, "And I'm getting really fucking tired of seeing his hands on you."

I bare my teeth at him, pushing out of his hold and backing up a step.

"I want to go home."

"Fern, please," my father says.

I'm shaking, "What else don't I know about my own life?"

"We thought–" my mother tries.

"No, you didn't. No one in this family has thought about me in two years!" I cry.

"We did it to keep you safe!" My father's voice booms over the commotion, "Let us explain, please."

His eyes look over my shoulder, and I turn, finding Noah's eyes, "You knew." He nods, and I feel like my whole world has shifted under me, "The phone call, it wasn't about the ranch."

"I was told to bring you home, but I said I didn't think you were ready to hear this news. I had no hand in any of it, by the time you arrived at the ranch, everythin' was already done," he lifts his hands to plead his innocence.

"Why?" My voice breaks with all the emotions clogging my brain.

No one answers me. I have a feeling this was not meant to be a public conversation, and my father confirms as much when he says, "Let's just enjoy our brunch, okay?"

My stomach rumbles and I charge past them to the glass doors of the restaurant. Hauling one of them open, I wait at the hostess stand. Crossing my arms over my chest feels like the only way to keep myself from falling apart.

I am married... to *Creed*.

The man I had drooled over...

Fantasized over...

Dreamed of...

So why does it feel like a horrible joke?

"Hi," the host says, jarring me from my thoughts, "Fern?"

The man looks familiar, in a way. I can't place his name, but his beard is trimmed neatly, and he is dressed in a pressed button down and slacks. His shoes are shiny, and his golden hair is slicked back and tapered on the sides.

"It's been a while," he says, walking toward me, "I'm Dean's little brother."

He approaches me, and I take a step back, straight into Creed's chest. Hands fall heavy on my shoulders and a deep voice sweeps over the room like a cool bucket of ice water, "Careful, Charmer."

"Don't call me that," I hiss, and shift my shoulders to shake

Creed's hands off.

"The reservation is under Hayes," he tells Dean's little brother, whose name I still can't remember.

"Of course," he scrambles back to the host stand and scans the tablet for our reservation. "This way."

Creed sweeps his arm out in front of me, and I stomp off in front of him. He chuckles, and I feel my cheeks heat. I hate the way his voice sends shivers up my spine, how my body heats at his proximity, and how my pulse has tripled.

I shouldn't want him, not after all the lies and half truths.

At our table I take the seat that faces the restaurant, I don't want my back to the door. The table is set with a menu at each place and glasses, already sweating with ice water in them.

The rest of the family files in, Creed on one side of me, Noah on the other. Manson across from us. The round table gives us the luxury of open communication.

"I want a divorce," I declare.

Creed laughs, "Not happening."

I turn, mouth open at his blatant refusal.

"I should have a say in who I'm going to spend the rest of my life with," I seethe through clenched teeth.

He leans down slowly, placing his lips just behind my ear. "You'll learn to love me," he whispers.

The waitress appears just as Creed leans away, when her eyes land on him, her smile brightens, and I roll my eyes.

"Hi all, my name is Lacy and I'll be your server today."

She's pretty, with her long brown hair tied up in a ponytail, and her uniform fits her like a glove. Her makeup is spot on, and I hate the way she smiles at all of us like we're all friends.

"Hi Lacy, I'll have a sweet tea," my mother starts the drink orders, like she always has, and we continue around the table until everyone's order is done. Her eyes linger on Creed, and it makes me want to laugh.

She walks away, ponytail swishing behind her as she goes.

"So, Noah," Creed starts, "How long are you planning on staying?"

I am also curious, will he be leaving soon? And if so, will I be able to go back too? I'm still not convinced that I want to stay here, especially with the person who murdered Gray being out and about.

"A few more days, I want to make sure Fern gets back into normal routines before I take off," he smiles at me, and I feel my heart sink a little. This isn't a visit, he lied to me.

"I think after today, we can manage," Creed says, drinking from his water glass. I watch his throat bob as he swallows. How the stubble there moves on his tanned skin.

"As her doctor, I won't leave until she shows significant

improvement," Noah challenges, "especially since this new development with her case."

"We've got that handled, she won't be receiving anymore notes," my father states.

"What? How can you possibly know that?" I ask.

That puzzle piece has to mean something, I didn't get a good look at it before, but I want to.

I need to.

"We turned it over to our private firm," my mother says, reaching across Creed and laying her hand on mine, "We won't let anything happen to you."

Lacy returns with our drinks and we all order, handing her our menus. Her hand brushes Creed's as he holds it up over his shoulder and I swear she swoons. I roll my eyes and murmur, "You can have him."

"What was that, darling?" Creed taunts.

"I said, I wanted to see it," I lie and smile.

He chuckles and Manson pipes up, "I took a picture of the drawing and the note for you, Ferny."

Creed's head swivels to his best friend. Manson unlocks his phone, "I can send it to you."

"I didn't bring my phone."

He nods and swipes on the screen before turning it around and handing it to me. The picture is extremely clear, but it isn't a whole image.

The puzzle piece must be part of a bigger message, it just looks like blurs of colors.

"Where's the rest?" I voice the question I'm sure everyone is thinking.

"We have it under control, sweetheart," my father assures me.

Conversation resumes, but I can't bring myself to contribute. I smile and nod, not really paying attention to what anyone is saying. Our food arrives and we eat. Manson laughs at something Candy says, and I excuse myself.

Creed eyes me, placing his hand on my wrist, "Where are you going?"

I jerk my hand out of his grip, "Bathroom."

He starts to stand, and I sigh, I don't need a babysitter. I need a moment to myself. To gather my thoughts and breathe.

"I can go to the bathroom alone, Creed."

He side-eyes me, but stands anyway. Leading us to the back of the restaurant, weaving in and out of the tables, to where the bathrooms are. I hate how big his presence is, everyone stares at us as we make our way through.

A table of men and women around my age are laughing and cutting up when we pass by, and I hear my name.

"Fern?" One of them yells.

"Holy shit, Fern Hayes! How the hell are you?" Another one says.

I look at them, trying to place their faces. The one I recognize as Garrett stands, crossing the space between us and gathering me up in his arms.

"We heard you left town, but shit Hayes. It's been what?" He looks back at the rest of the table, "Two years?"

His sister, Gretchen, scoffs from her seat between her brother and Dean.

"Yeah," I say, trying to push out of his embrace. His arms are circled around my hips, and all I want is for him to back off.

"Remove your hands from my wife," Creed's voice was low, deadly. Like a whip cracked to get a horse moving.

Garrett backs up and looks between the two of us to my hand.

"Married, huh?" Dean parrots, standing up from the table, "Who would have thought? Congrats, Creed."

His dark eyes travel down the length of my arm, zeroing in on the empty finger attached to my body.

I huff and push Creed out of my way. He stands there a moment longer than necessary as I push the door to the ladies room open. I knew both Dean and Garrett knew

Creed and Manson, they palled around a few times before, but the whole interaction left me confused and a bit put-off. The way they all eyed Creed and I, as if they know our 'marriage' is a sham.

Heading for the sink I splash cold water on my face and let it trail down, dripping on my shirt. I don't want to do this anymore, I hate pretending that everything is normal, that I'm the same Fern who allowed people to touch me whenever they wanted.

Creed stomps into the bathroom, and I jump.

"You will not allow anyone else to put their hands on you, anymore," he growls. "And I don't like the way that fuckwit looked at you."

I've had it.

"You don't get to make those demands," I shout, as he steps into my space. "You don't get to be my bodyguard, you don't get to be my jailer. You aren't anyone significant to me, you're just the man who I was sold to, and I won't let you tell me what I can and cannot do!"

"Charmer, do not push me," he warns.

"Then stay away from me," I challenge.

He steps closer and I take a step back, his smile reveals his striking teeth and as I take another step back I realize he's backed me into the sink. The cool quartz countertop digging into my lower back as his stomach brushes my chest and his arms cage me in.

"I can't stay away from you. You're mine now, and I'll die before I let anything happen to you again," his breath smells like mint despite having eaten. "I don't want to see anyone else's hands on what's mine. Understand?"

"You don't even love me, Creed. I'm your possession."

The realization hits me, this isn't about love for him. It's about keeping me safe, but what kind of life can I truly have in a loveless marriage, trapped in a gilded cage?

"How would you know?" He leans in closer, as if there's much space to begin with.

My breaths stall and my chest gets tight, his leather and sandalwood scent over take my senses and I gasp. He's so close I can see all the colors that make up his green eyes, the yellows and navy ring around the edge.

His lips are invitingly pink and look soft, surrounded by dark scruff that's trimmed perfectly. His eyes dip to my lips and flutters erupt in my stomach. I duck under Creed's arm, "I'll be out in a minute."

His face turns to stone, but he doesn't move, just crosses his arms over his chest and waits.

We stand there, eyeing each other. Neither one of us is willing to give in to the other. We're at a stalemate.

"I'm going to throw up," I try.

"Don't care," he smirks.

"I have to shit."

He laughs. "Again, don't care."

"Why can't you let me have two minutes?" I ask, closing my eyes and wishing for him to leave.

"Because, Charmer, I don't trust you."

"Oh, that's rich coming from you," I accuse. "What with all the honesty you've been giving me."

He smirks, "You weren't ready yet, and judging by your childish reaction, I was right."

"My childish reaction?" my eyes have to be bugging out of my head, "I was told I had a husband, and not just any husband, but my brother's best friend. You knew I had a crush on you before everything went to shit, and you're standing there telling me I had a childish reaction?"

"How else would you describe it?"

"A sane woman's reaction," I throw my hands up in exasperation. "I've been married off to a man I don't know anymore, for years, without my consent, and everyone just seems to be okay with it."

"I'm the same person I was when 'everything went to shit' as you so eloquently put it."

"No you aren't," I argue.

"Whatever you need to tell yourself, Fern. Either use the fucking toilet or leave, but I'm not going anywhere."

I spin on my heel and walk out, he's infuriating, and too casual about everything going on.

I still don't have the whole picture, I know it deep in my bones.

Just like I know I won't get those answers until I play into whatever Creed has planned.

I only hope my heart can take it.

Chapter Fifteen

The rest of brunch is the same, everyone making casual conversation, Dean and Garrett come over to say goodbye and offer to get together to catch up.

We weren't super close before the incident, so I don't think too much into it. I have no intentions of hanging out with them anyway.

My dad claps his hands together and says, "Are you ready for the next bit?"

I can see how excited he is, and I just can't bring myself to tell him no. He's trying, going as far as declining to speak to some influential people who had arrived during our brunch.

"Lay it on me."

I nod and smile like I know they want me to. Manson and Candy look at each other, and I feel a pang of sadness. We had that, Manson and I. Even Candy and I had that silent way of communicating once upon a time.

I am jealous, plain and simple. They were mine before

they were each others'.

But, then everything happened and well, I just couldn't function anymore.

"We're going to the farmers market downtown," Candy says, excitement lacing her tone, and I have a sneaking suspicion that it isn't just for flowers like we used to do.

"Do they still have those honeycombs on sticks?" I ask her.

She smiles, popping her dimples, and nods her head.

"Okay, I'm in."

She mouths a 'thank you' my way and it feels genuine. Maybe a few things from the old me never changed. Flowers and honeycombs were mine and Candy's ritual on Saturday mornings.

We would get up early just so we could get to the flower stand first. Marty always sold out of his peonies, and I hated not having fresh flowers in my room.

Noah stands up with me and whispers, "It's okay to say no."

I look at him and nod. I know what he means, that my family will understand if I don't want to push myself. That I need to work at *my* pace.

When we get to the SUV, Creed is waiting on the bench seat, arm relaxed over the back headrests, and my parents are nowhere to be found.

He raises his eyebrows as I seethe at him, "Those peonies won't be there long if you keep staring at me."

My mouth pops open, how did he know? Does he really pay that much attention, or did Candy tell him?

Either way, I slide into the cab and lean into Noah so I won't touch Creed.

Even though he keeps his eyes on me the whole drive.

The market is packed, so the driver drops us off at the entrance, promising to park and telling us to call when we are ready to leave.

The three of us make our way into the market. People are everywhere, chatting and laughing with vendors and patrons.

It's everything I remembered. There are a few more stalls, but almost everything is exactly where it ought to be.

Marty is standing beside his flower display speaking to a customer when his eyes land on mine.

"My word!" He exclaims, excusing himself from the woman to stride over to me. He wraps his arms around my shoulders and spins me around, "Fern, look at you!"

My cheeks heat and I turn away from him for a moment. Creed is there, eyes heavy on Marty's arms locked around my waist, and I smirk. Because he doesn't need to know

Marty is gay, or that he's happily married.

"Come, come!"

Marty links his fingers in mine and leads me to his stall where he has peonies waiting in a bundle. White peonies, my favorite. I scoop up the bundle and inhale, they are beautiful, silky smooth petals in a creamy vanilla shade, barely opened yet. Their stems are bright green, and I tear up.

"Your friend called," Marty says, nodding to Candy.

A lone tear slides down my cheek as my family watches, it feels healing in a way. To cry tears of joy.

I scan the stall, all the bright colors soothing something inside me. Creams, blush, red, blue, purple, yellow. I scoop up a bundle of the brightest sunflowers and wink at Marty. Walking to Candy, I hand her the flowers and throw my arms around her.

"I'm so sorry, Fern," her voice slips in and out, "I never forgave myself for what happened, fuck."

We laugh as our tears fall.

"We'll work on it," I promise.

"Who wants honeycomb?" Manson's voice enters our little circle. I hadn't even seen him slip away. "What did I miss?"

We all laugh and Candy hugs me tighter. It isn't complete

forgiveness, but it will be, eventually.

I loop my arm through hers and we set off, walking down the aisles and buying anything that catches our fancy. It feels normal, like déjá vu.

My flowers are getting hot in my hand as we walk further and further into the market, so I unlink our arms to switch hands. Something hard pricks my finger, but peonies don't have thorns.

"Hold on," I whisper to Candy, flicking my eyes up to where Manson and Creed are following behind.

I undo the wide band that keeps the stems together, and out tumbles what looks like a small envelope from the florist, when you get flowers delivered. The card is white, but flecked with red.

Bending down to pick it up, I feel something with hard edges inside.

It can't be...

"Fern.." someone says.

Creed's tattooed hand snatches the envelope from my hand. He rips the card open and runs his tongue along his bottom lip.

"We need to leave," he tells Manson. "Call the cars."

Manson does as he is asked, immediately calling Jax on his phone.

"Wait a second," I place my hand on Creed's, "Let me see it."

"No," he growls, eyes hard and face set in a grim line.

"Yes."

He faces me fully, staring me down just like in the bathroom earlier, "No."

I grip the paper and yank, another puzzle piece hits the pavement without a sound. Though it has to make a sound, right? I can't hear anything, like my ears just quit working.

My eyes find Creed's and he looks pissed, but doesn't comment. Instead he picks the piece up and pockets both it and the note. My flowers have fallen, and are now strewn all over the ground.

"Come on," Creed grips my hand and tugs me along, "I'll buy you more."

We make it to the car, and once again I find myself sandwiched between Noah and Creed. I can't keep my legs still as we drive, and I shake them up and down while I chew on my lip.

When we finally make it back to the house, I follow Creed out of the SUV. I want answers, I want to know what the note said this time, Creed, Manson, and Noah all follow my dad into his office.

When I enter, Creed demands I leave.

"There's nothing you can do," he barks.

"I want to know what it says." I stand as tall as I can, brushing my body against his.

"I won't ask you again, Fern," he grinds out between tightly clenched teeth, "Let us do what we need to do, alone."

"This is about me damn it!" I fume, I'm sick of being left out, and having to shout to be heard.

Creed's eyes zero in on me and he smiles. It's feral, and I take a step back.

"Excuse us, Mr. Hayes," his voice is still growly, "But Mrs. Hemlock and I need to have a chat."

"No, we..." I begin as he lifts me around my middle and hauls me over his shoulder. "What the *fuck*, Creed. Put me down."

He doesn't say anything as we pass my mom and Candy in the living room, their stares a mix of worry and confusion. He carries me up the stairs, careful not to bounce me too much, straight to my room where he throws me on the bed and kicks the door shut.

"Let's get a few things straight, *wife*," he stalks over to the bed where I'm sprawled out in shock at how he just manhandled me. "One, if there is anything you need to know, I'll tell you," he sticks his fingers up like I can't count on my own, "Two, if you continue to push my patience, I *will* snap, and it won't be pretty. Three, if you ever–*and I mean ever*–get another note like this, I need you to bring it to *me* first, no questions asked."

The note is between the fingers he holds up, and it takes everything in me not to launch myself at him so I can read it.

"Okay, *husband*," I spit. "Let me clue you in." I sit up on my knees against the edge of the bed, and even then I still don't reach his height, "If you don't tell me what the note says I'll go to the police and hand over every shred of evidence I have against this psychopath. Then I'll contact a lawyer and have divorce papers drawn up and signed in no time."

I wait, chest heaving and face stone.

He laughs in my face, running his hand down over his beard.

"That was cute, darling, and you know what?" He leans down into my space, our eyes locked, noses touching, lips millimeters away from each other, "I dare you to try."

Chapter Sixteen

"What?"

"You heard me, sweetheart," he backs away to the door, pulling it open and slipping out. I can't move.

I can try.

I can *try?*

This man is calling my bluff.

The new phone I left here this morning lights up and I smile, oh I'd be contacting a lawyer alright.

I pick up the device noting the screen protector and case. It's plain, but the tempered glass is heavily tinted, like a privacy screen. Perfect.

Swiping the phone open, I'm greeted with notifications, a few texts from people who have heard I'm home, and one missed call. It was a blocked number, and they left a voicemail.

Ignoring the notifications, I click on the internet, searching for a lawyer that I know never worked for any of the Hayes'. I can't be sure of the Hemlock name, but I have to try. The office is still open, and I smile.

Quickly walking down the stairs I swipe the keys to my old car. I haven't driven in a while, but that doesn't mean I don't know how. Popping open the driver side door I slide in, the black leather seats are cool, and it smells like a faint reminder of the girl I once was.

I knew the second they heard the door open they would come running, so I start the engine and hit the garage door button on my visor. It slowly rises, and since my car is the last in the bay it takes them a moment to get through the house to try and stop me.

The GPS says it will take twenty minutes to get there, so I put the car in reverse and hit the gas once the door is lifted enough for my little car to get through. Muffled voices carry as I crank the wheel and shift my car into drive.

Creed is the first to hit the empty space where my car usually sits, followed by Manson and then my dad. They are all yelling, and when I look in my rearview mirror I see Noah. Smart, he went out the front door. But even he can't stop my foot from smashing the gas pedal to the floor.

Pebbles spray as the wheels gain traction, and the car speeds off. I take a deep breath, knowing I'm doing this for me. That I am taking control of something in my life. I'm so tired of being told to sit quietly while the police do nothing in Gray's case, this is no different, and I won't sit idle.

The drive isn't bad, I crank the volume on the radio and roll my windows down. When I arrive at the office building I find the closest parking spot and put the car in park. The building is next to the court house, gray stone with white accents.

I shove my phone into my back pocket and swirl my keys around one finger.

I can do this.

The glass door is immaculate, and makes me want to smudge my hand on it. I restrain myself, and approach the ladies at the front desk. They both have their hair swept up into a ballerina type bun, minimal makeup, and a slim build.

"Do you have an appointment?" One of them asks.

"Actually, I don't," I tell her, "However, if Mr. Fontine could see me for five minutes, I would be grateful."

The two look at each other, and the one who asked if I had an appointment chews on the inside of her cheek.

"I'm sorry, but without an appointment I'm afraid he won't be able to help you."

"I figured as much, but could you tell him my name? Maybe I could leave my phone number?"

"Sure," she smiles, handing me a piece of heavy card stock

and a pen.

I write my name and have to pull out my phone to find my new number. Once done, I hand her the paper, with my name clearly visible on the card. "Thank you," I say over my shoulder as I start walking out.

"Fern Hayes?" one of them gasps, "The one from that guy's murder." They aren't very quiet as they whisper to each other, and I flinch.

"The mayor's daughter is here," I hear the other one, presumably on the phone with Mr. Fontine.

Before I can reach for the handle on the front door the one on the phone shouts for me to wait. I pause, turning around slowly and spotting Mr. Fontine as he exits his office. He is a middle aged man with white hair and an outdated sense of fashion.

But he has great ratings as a divorce attorney, and he doesn't look like a sleazy man after young women.

"Miss. Hayes, I'm Fontine, how can I help you?"

"Could we talk in your office? I promise not to take up much of your time," I smile, and wink at the girls as I follow him to the back of the building.

"Please, sit," he offers before sitting behind his desk and placing his hands together on top of the lacquered wood.

"Thank you," I have no idea where to start so I just

jump straight to the point, "I need a divorce, with as much discretion as possible."

His eyes grow wide and his brows furrow, "Oh."

He looks at his computer, and asks me a few questions, namely who I am married to.

"Creed Hemlock."

Mr. Fontine's face turns white, draining of color when I say Creed's name. He looks at me and says something I don't expect, "Forgive me, Mrs. Hemlock, but I can't help you, and I doubt any lawyer on this side of the continent will either."

"Excuse me?" I question, he can't mean that.

"I've never met your husband, but I can tell you his family will have my head if I do this," he gulps and continues, "I have children, Mrs. Hemlock. I can't—no, I won't, participate in anything remotely close to that family."

I let my eyes travel the room as this information tickles a memory I had forgotten. Creed was sent to his brother's to learn their line of work, but no one could ever tell me exactly what they did.

Any time I'd ask Manson he'd find some reason not to answer. There is something I'm missing and until I know what it is there is no point prolonging the poor man's misery by begging him to help me.

"I understand, Mr. Fontine," I stand, and cross the room

showing myself out.

Once I emerge from the office and click the button on my key fob, I unlock the door and slide into my seat.

What the fuck am I going to do now?

A car pulls into the parking lot, windows tinted and body sleek with a custom wrap that had to have cost a fortune. It pulls in behind me effectively blocking my car into the spot.

Fear coats my insides.

I can't see the driver, I don't know how many people are in the car, and I have just lost my quick getaway. The driver's side opens and a booted foot steps out. I close my eyes, terrified to see anything else.

When the door closes with a loud bang I look back up into my mirror to find Creed stalking to my door. I turn my head away and pretend to be looking at my phone. I don't want Creed targeting the man who tried to help me.

He refused anyway.

I quickly delete my history and clear my trash before he knocks on the window, and tries the handle but I'm not stupid, I locked the car the moment my door closed.

"Charmer, open the door," he demands.

I turn and face him, it's getting dark and my own windows are slightly tinted, so I can't make out all of his features, but I know he's pissed.

The two receptionists walk out, eyeing Creed and I as they pass. They don't stop, in fact they start walking faster. What happened to helping fellow women out?

"No."

He hits the window with his palm, "Open. The fucking. Door."

"No."

I start the car, and he taps a few buttons on his phone. My car turns off, and I fumble with the button to reignite the engine.

That psychopath has remote access to my car.

I hate him.

"I can stand here all night, Charmer," he says, waving his phone in front of my window, "But the longer you take to open the door the more trouble you'll be in."

"Should I be worried?" I quip.

"Depends on what you're doing here."

"I told you what I would do," I shrug, and Mr. Fontine emerges from the glass doors of his building.

Creed follows my line of sight and spots him.

"Ah," he chuckles, "Well, his blood will be on your hands then."

His strides are purposeful and even as he crosses the parking lot, approaching Mr. Fontine, I can see the menace taut in his posture. I pull the handle on my door and push it open, hurrying to get between them.

"Okay," I heave, "I'm out, what do you want?"

"I want to know what Mr. Fontine here had to say to my wife."

Fontine blanches, even more so than when I was in his office, "N-nn-nothing, sir. I told her I wouldn't do what she wanted."

"Good," Creed nods, "What else?"

"Nothing, I swear," he cries.

"We're leaving," Creed grips my arm as I try to turn and apologize to Mr. Fontine. He spins me around and walks me to his SUV.

He lifts me into the passenger seat and buckles me in, shutting the door and then turning around to shut and lock my car. I unbuckle and open the door to get out.

"If you step one fucking foot outside of my car I will spank your ass so hard you wont be able to walk tomorrow."

My eyes flick to his, and fuck if it doesn't do something to me. He picks my keys up off the ground where I'd dropped them in my pursuit of saving Mr. Fontine, never breaking eye contact.

"Shut the goddamn door, Fern," he lashes.

I sullenly do as he says, watching him walk around the

front of the SUV and open the door. He slides in with a lethal grace only he can achieve. I can practically hear his teeth grinding, and see the way a vein in his forehead has popped.

"Why can't you just accept that I'm trying to help you?"

"Because I can help myself."

"Obviously," he scoffs.

"How would you feel, Creed? Coming back years after damn near dying, and learning major decisions in your life have been made for you?"

He doesn't answer, just starts the car and peels out of the lot.

"I could've driven myself home," I grumble.

He still doesn't speak as he drives, the whole way back gripping the steering wheel like he wants to strangle it.

"Were you in love with him?" He finally speaks when we pull up in front of my house.

"Who?"

"Grayson Lansing."

I haven't heard his name said out loud in so long it feels like a punch to the gut.

"No," I answer honestly.

"And your doctor?"

I scoff, "I'm not answering that."

Not only is it not his business, it's something Noah would

be insulted by. Something *I* am insulted by. I unbuckle my seat belt and open the car door, slamming it behind me.

I walk into the house, and straight up the stairs, where Noah is waiting in my room.

"I don't feel like talking." I say as I quietly close my door, leaning against it and breathing out heavily.

"You don't have to talk about Creed, but we should discuss what happened at the market."

"Unless you're going to tell me what that note said, I don't want to talk."

He sighs, "it said, *you won't get away from me this time*."

I spin around, eyeing him. He is serious, and I take a steadying breath. So many things are running through my mind, questions and puzzles.

"Why would Creed want to hide that from me?"

"Fern, I think you're forgetting that your family experienced this outside of you. You were attacked, along with your then boyfriend, and Creed was the one who found you in the woods. He said he thought you were dead. Your head wound was deep, he thought you had bled out before he got there."

"When your brother found out, he refused to leave you. He's been seeing a therapist along with Candy, and nine times out of ten that night is the topic of conversation," he runs a hand through his hair. "Then, after Manson found you on the bathroom floor, Candy had to perform CPR on you. Fern, when you got out of the hospital, you took too many of your prescription pain meds with little to no regard for what might happen, and who may be affected. Your parents didn't know what to do, so when they contacted me I told them that the best treatment for you would be no contact. It was the easiest transition for you at the time, but they had to keep living, your dad is the mayor for goodness sake."

It was hard to hear these things. I'd known that life for the people I loved went on while I was at the farm, but I had no idea that it had been Noah keeping them from contacting me.

"Your mother stopped going to a lot of her functions, the police asked them question after question that even I couldn't help answer, even after months of you being at the ranch. Give them credit, and a little grace. I'm not saying you have to forgive them, that's going to come in time, but maybe try to see all of their perspectives."

I hadn't thought about it in those terms, this whole time I just thought of my pain and trauma. I didn't even consider the shit they went through.

Does that make me a bad person?

Selfish?

"I...had no idea." Everything Noah said was true, I haven't been giving anyone any grace. I have been so focused on me, that I didn't consider what they also went through. I need to journal all of my thoughts, and try to focus them into something I can understand.

Noah stands, handing me a new journal and wishing me a good night.

Chapter Seventeen

I write for what feels like hours, skipping dinner so I can continue writing. I'm not hungry anyway. Manson brings me a covered plate and leaves it on my nightstand. We don't speak, he just gives me a nod as I sit in my chair, legs curled up under me with my journal on my knees and my pen flying across the page.

Everything I'm thinking bleeds out into the page. I have to get it out while it is all fresh, and once I'm finally done I leave it on the chair and undress. Feeling lighter than I have in a while, I start the shower.

After, I lather on lotion and complete my skin care routine. A new robe hangs on the back of my door and when I slip it on, I hug myself.

The material is butter smooth, and whispers against my skin. The steam from my shower has evaporated some, but when I open the bathroom door cool air still blows in. It feels amazing and I soak it in.

I'd forgotten how I had once felt in this house.

Shutting off the lights I crawl into bed, exhaustion from everything today pulling me under, and I sleep dreamlessly.

I wake with my pulse pounding, and skin sweaty. Even though I put on a tank top and shorts, I'm still lying in a pool of sweat. Desire and lust run rampant through my veins, but I can't remember having any dreams.

I am so turned on my pussy is practically throbbing. It's been a while since I've touched myself, and over two years since I've had sex.

Twisting so I can crawl to the edge of the bed, I slide open the drawer on my nightstand. I'm surprised to find all of my things still here, cleaned. Embarrassment heats my cheeks thinking of someone cleaning my sex toys.

I hit the power button on one to see if it's charged, and the light blinks once and stays. Vibrations immediately begin, and I groan at the memories of pleasure.

Crawling back into the middle of the bed, I lean back against the headboard. Splaying my legs wide and running the buzzing toy over the fabric that covers my pussy.

An orgasm will give me enough endorphins to fall asleep, a happier drug than chemicals.

I stroke the toy up and down a few times, easing my body into the feeling once again. Closing my eyes, I use my other hand to slowly pull my tank top up and over my breasts. Letting them spill out on either side of my chest. My nipples draw up and pebble into hard peaks.

Bringing the toy up, I circle my nipples, feeling another spark of hunger radiate through my limbs. Wiggling out of my shorts, I kick the sheets down my legs and expose myself to the emptiness of my room.

Thoughts of Creed creep into my head, the way his body touched mine, his threat of spanking me.

Slowly I move the toy to my dripping cunt, imagining his tattooed hands on my breast instead of my own. The way his voice would go growly when he finally touches me.

I groan, feeling the way the toy stretches my body. The vibrations are small, but with every thrust the toy hits my clit just right and my legs shake.

"Charmer."

I startle, pulling the toy from my body and whimpering. I may be very good at conjuring his voice in my mind, but there's no way that was in my head. The nickname only he uses, the same one that drives me insane when he uses it.

He's in my room, although I can't see him. I gulp, trying to calm my racing heart, while I scan the room, failing to pinpoint him.

"C-Creed?" I stutter into the dark, just in case I am going out of my mind and imagining it.

"Please, continue." A shadow moves in my right view, "Show me how you used to let him fuck you."

"What?" I whisper.

He doesn't answer, instead his shadow moves closer to the edge of my bed, fear registers in my brain, along with anticipation, sending all the fine hairs rising on my body.

I'm not scared of Creed. He would never hurt me, I know it like I know my very bones.

He casually sits on the bench at the foot of my bed, and I instinctively close my legs.

"You shouldn't be here." I purr, finally finding the courage to put more than one word together.

"Open your legs and show me what belongs to me," he rumbles out.

I shouldn't.

I really, *really* shouldn't, because Creed isn't the man I used to know. He looks like him, but older...different.

Harder.

Like he could kill a man with his bare hands and not think twice about it.

Plus I'm still angry that we are technically married and I had no say in it whatsoever.

"You should leave," I manage around heavy breaths, dropping the toy to the bed.

One of his shoulders lifts, but I can't see his face to gauge what he is thinking. I shift in the bed, twisting my legs so I can sit up higher.

His hand whips out, like a crack of lighting, clamping around my ankle.

"Show. Me." The depth to which his voice sinks sends panic rushing through my system, along with wetness between my thighs.

I don't understand why my body reacts to him. Why his touch ignites a simmering boil under my skin, not an immediate flight reaction. I *want* him to touch me, I *want* his eyes on me. I have wanted it for so long that now that I have it, I don't know what to do with it.

As if all this time away has made me...shy.

"You need to leave," the words rush out. My thoughts are churning as he tugs on my leg, opening me back up for his viewing pleasure. He stands, hovering over my bed. The toy starts buzzing between his fingers, he must've picked it up when I dropped it. He runs it along my side, over the dips and valleys of my flesh.

"Tell me, did he fuck you the way you like?"

The way he asks has my heart hammering in my chest. I don't know exactly who he's referring to, but I can hazard a guess.

"Did he know how you like to be fucked?" He asks again, worded differently, as if I might not understand. Contained anger slithers low in my gut, I am not incompetent.

"Wouldn't you like to know how I like to be fucked." I state, sitting straight up and meeting his frame that's still positioned over my bed, "Why are you even here?" Our eyes are aligned now, I can see every feature of his handsome face, "You've never even paid me a second glance."

He laughs, the dark and twisted sort, "I've spent my life *hating* that all I've ever done is watch you, Charmer," his eyes narrow.

"You're lying," I spit. Creed is a great many things, but he has never been a liar. The thought sours my tongue as he continues his assault on my body.

"Listen to me very carefully, Fern," his voice is sharp and deadly, "I've spent the entirety of my existence trying *not* to want my best friend's little sister."

"This isn't funny, Creed," I whimper as he moves the toy to

my pussy, and the movements strike a match in me, "Don't you think I've been through enough?"

Tears threaten to spill over. I've wanted Creed for so many years and he knows it too, so if this is a joke, it's cruel, even for him.

"I know what you did that night. I know you were fucking your daddy's publicist. Just like I know, anytime you fucked him or anyone else, you imagined it was *me*."

My jaw drops, Gray and I were careful, never meeting at public places until...the party. But Creed couldn't have seen him, couldn't have followed us, I heard the party in the background when I called him.

I'm sure of it.

"You're a bastard!" I shout, launching myself out of bed away from him and toward the bathroom door. My hands are slick from sweat and I struggle with the lock.

Hands circle my waist as he lifts me off the floor and throws me back onto the bed. He flips me over so I'm on my back. His body cages mine in, I am not a small girl, and I have only gained muscle since working on the farm. The fact that he can just toss me around is as heady as it is terrifying.

"We've already established that, Charmer."

His hands dig into my hips, bruising the flesh there, and I remember I am half naked. His body comes down on mine, arms held beside my head so he won't completely crush me. I am at his mercy.

This Creed, I don't recognize.

This Creed, I *am* scared of.

Terror bubbles up like hot lava about to erupt, "Get off me."

"You think I don't watch you," his lips graze my ear as he continues. "That I don't want you, why is that, Fern?" He angles his head to look at me, beard brushing my chin and neck.

"Because…" I start, but I can feel his cock straining through his jeans.

"Say it."

"No. Just because you're hard doesn't mean you want *me*. You just want to fuck me. Then what, huh? You've had your best friend's little sister, add that trophy to your bedpost?"

He barks a laugh, making the bulge in his jeans rub against my center, "You keep telling yourself that, and one day it might be true."

I struggle against him, feeling the way his legs clench around my hips and thighs, caging me in tighter than before.

"If that's all you want, you can go to hell."

"I know you want me, just as much as I want you," he smiles against my cheek, "I found a way to save you, make sure your family isn't targeted, and keep you all for myself."

"I'm not yours to keep," I hiss at him as he lifts off me and saunters toward the door. His footsteps impossibly light on my soft carpet.

"We'll see about that."

It's the last thing he says before he leaves me half naked and confused. The toy is still buzzing on the mattress, but I am no longer in the mood to do anything. My brain is scrambled, and I just want to sleep.

His words play on repeat in my head, and I try not to over analyze them, but I can't take any chances where Creed Hemlock is concerned.

I need straight answers, and if he won't give them to me, I know a certain brother, who will.

Chapter Eighteen

Sleeping in my bed after Creed was here proves futile, and I know if I am going to catch Manson alone, I need to be up early anyway.

He used to go for a run every morning, so I am placing all my bets on him returning soon. Standing on the back patio with a cup of coffee—and a blanket wrapped around my shoulders since it's chillier than I expected—I bide my time.

I watch the tree line, waiting for him to emerge, sweaty and gross. Sipping my coffee I hum at the warmth that travels down my body. On cue, Manson appears at the beginning of the trail he created.

He doesn't spot me until he looks up at the house while unlocking the gate. He pops his ear buds out and smiles.

"Hey, Ferny."

I smile back; it's the second time I've heard him use my nickname since coming back. The simpleness of the gesture tugs at my heart.

"Can I ask you something?" I say, clearing my throat.

"Anything," he looks eager to be having this conversation, and I guess I am too because I haven't spoken to him in two years.

"Why did mom and dad marry me off?"

"Uh," he swallows, "Have you talked to Creed about it?"

"No offense, but you pick hard friends to be around."

He barks out a laugh, "You aren't wrong," his eyes soften as he looks at me. He sits on the seat next to where I stand and asks, "Will you sit down with me?"

I nod and sit, "Please Manson, I feel like I'm going insane with everything I don't know. Plus this maniac is still out there somewhere, what if they break in and finish what they started? And I can't defend myself because I don't know all the details."

Sucking in a deep breath Manson leans back in his chair, eyes looking out at the tree line and immaculately kept yard.

"They wanted Creed to testify about what he saw that night, and because he was the first one on the scene, he could describe it," he rubs his hand on the back of his neck.

"And? Now I'm shackled to him for life? Because he could describe the crime scene?"

He shakes his head and looks at his lap, "There's

something you don't remember, and no one has told you yet. Something else happened that night."

"What do you mean?" My hands are shaking, even though I try to hide them under the blanket.

"There was another body. The police thought you killed her, and they were building a case against *you*."

Shock spirals through my body, "What?"

"I thought he would tell you, or maybe you would remember, but when you never said anything to anyone, including Noah, the police wanted him to testify against you."

"Wait, I'm still processing the second murder," I hold up a palm because what the fuck? "Who's body was it?"

"Jane Doe," he shrugs, "No one has claimed her, or made a missing persons report, and she wasn't in any of the federal systems."

"Why would they think I killed her? I was bleeding, and running for my life." I couldn't have, I didn't see anyone else that night, or I would have asked them for help.

"Because she was stabbed with your keys," I don't hear the door open, or Creed's footsteps, so I jump up when I spot him, standing on my toes.

"How much have you heard?" Manson asks, looking at Creed.

"Enough, I can take it from here." He nods toward the house and Manson stands, clapping him on the back as he passes.

Well, that's problematic.

I don't have time to be concerned about last night, I am too busy. Trying to dig deeper into my thoughts, to remember that night. We stand there in silence as he lets me process.

"Sit," he commands and I do, because I want answers.

"Do you remember the trip I took after Manson and I graduated?" He asks, and it feels like it came from left field.

"What does that–"

"Do you remember?" He interrupts.

I nod.

"It was more than my brother showing me the ropes of our business, it was an..." He sighs, "Initiation, for lack of better terms."

"Okay."

"There's a lot you don't know about me, and before I tell you about New York, I need to know if you're with me, because once I tell you, there is no out."

"With you," I test the words, feeling how they surface, "You mean, be *Mrs. Hemlock.*"

"It means a lot more than that, Charmer. I came to talk to

you your first night back, but you were asleep."

"And yet, you stayed," I fire back.

"And yet, I stayed," he nods, "Fern, I wasn't lying to you last night. I would never lie to you."

"So you're what… saying you're in love with me?" I scoff, in what world?

His eyes bore into mine, his face serious, "I could be."

Breath leaves my lungs in a rush, he's saying he could love me, that the seed is already there. That we could be *in love* with each other.

"Creed."

"I don't know if I can give you forever, but I can damn sure try."

Thoughts die on my tongue as I search his face, he's serious.

"Forever… with me."

He nods, "With you."

"What if I can't love you?"

He smirks, "I think you can be persuaded."

"*Creed.*"

"Okay," he says, leaning back in the seat Manson was sitting in, legs splayed wide. "My family's business isn't exactly a legal venture, so are you in this with me or not?"

"I'm in dammit, now stop speaking in riddles and just tell

me."

"My father is the head of the mafia on the east coast."

My mouth drops open, and I laugh. It's not a cute laugh, it's manic and borderline hysterical, "Okay, so like guns, drugs, skin? Oh God, don't tell me you're human traffickers."

My brain is working overtime to process the things he hasn't said.

"Calm down, Charmer," he leans his elbows on his knees and I stand. Pacing back and forth in front of him seems like the best course of action right now.

"Tell me you aren't swiping people off the streets and selling them to the highest bidder," I almost plead.

His smile is laced with mirth as he looks at me, "So you're not worried about my brothers or me possibly inheriting the mafia, just if we buy and sell people?"

I stop and stare at him, "You're going to be a mob boss?"

He rolls his eyes, "That's generally what happens when the leader retires, or dies."

"But your brother..."

He shakes his head, "We don't know who he will name."

"Who?"

"Our father," he stands in front of me, our bodies aligned, "Charmer, tell me now if you can't do this with me. I'll still help you find this stalker, I swear, but I can't stay if you won't even try to build a life with me."

"Because you're in love with me."

"Utterly obsessed," he smiles.

Stepping up to him I hold out my hand, "Okay."

"I promise you won't regret me," he says gently. Taking my hand and tugging me close to press our foreheads together.

Pulling away and looking up at him I ask, "So, if your dad picks you to run the mob, will that make me like, the First Lady?"

"How about I promise to answer all of your questions over breakfast?"

"Deal."

He follows me inside to the kitchen, where Candy and Manson are currently making out.

"I was so not prepared to deal with this." I declare as they split apart.

"I'm sorry," Candy's lips are red and her neck flushed, "We didn't hear you come in."

"It's fine, but could you maybe not eat each other's faces in common areas of the house?"

Manson laughs and plants a kiss on Candy's cheek, promising to return after a shower. She finishes whatever it is she started cooking while I cut up some fruit for myself and put on a pot of water.

Creed moves around the kitchen as if he lives here too. Which is one of my many questions.

He whisks together eggs and cheese, pouring it into a hot skillet, and I watch the muscles in his back shift as he stirs the eggs around.

"You gonna get this water, Charmer?" He throws over his shoulder and I snap out of staring at the hypnotizing way he moves. Pulling the boiling water off the stove I add in the instant oatmeal I've grown to love, letting it thicken. Then I add in the freshly cut strawberries and plate it up.

I left some for Noah, knowing it will give him a sense of home.

Creed raises his brow, and I roll my eyes at him.

"You don't get to be jealous."

Now both his brows rise and I stifle a laugh, walking to the patio once more.

We sit in silence for a while, him with his pile of scrambled eggs, and me with my oatmeal. The birds chirp in the distance, and I can still hear the grasshoppers singing.

Thoughts and questions swirl in my head, I blow on my oatmeal, cooling it off before eating a big spoonful.

"I never took you for an oatmeal girl."

"I didn't know body builders could have cheese."

"Touché," he chuckles and drinks a hearty swallow of

orange juice.

Full body shivers erupt in my body, orange juice and eggs...gross. I watch him shovel his eggs into his mouth, and then immediately swallow more orange juice. It was like a horror movie you don't want to watch, but you do it anyway because you don't want to miss something.

"Alright," he says, swallowing the last of his juice and wiping his mouth on a napkin, "I can see the cogs working in your brain."

"I have so many questions, I don't know which to ask first."

Honestly I really don't, I still need to know the reason he had to marry me while I was incapacitated in the hospital. Then there's the mafia. Forget it, my brain is mush—like the pile of oatmeal I just destroyed—and I don't want to miss anything. But I'm married to the guy, I can ask him anything, anytime I want, right?

"This isn't like a one time tell-all right?" I ask him.

"You have me until death, I'm sure there will be questions between now and then," he smirks.

"Okay," I nod and eat the last bite of oatmeal from my bowl. Swallowing it down, I immediately jump into my original question, "speaking of, having you 'til death, why exactly did you have to marry me?"

"One of two reasons, and I can't answer the second part right now, so don't ask."

Damn, refusal right out of the gate. This was going to go swimmingly.

"Manson told you about the other body, and that the police wanted me to testify. Well, as husband and wife, I legally cannot be forced to testify against you, and that works out for everyone, because I did a lot of damage control that night."

"Damage control?"

"Part of the second reason," he grumbles.

I got the sense that he wasn't thrilled about the second reason, and it made me even more curious.

"How did you get us married so quickly? It had to have been less than twenty-four hours."

He eyes me then, because I know the answer, and he can't voice it.

"Mafia, got it. Here's the thing though," this is the part that I can't figure out on my own, "My parents, do they know about you?"

He nods and grabs our empty plates.

"Manson?" I twist my body so I can watch him carrying the dishes back into the house. He stops mid stride and nods.

I need my journal, but can I even write about this? If it fell into the wrong hands it would be...troublesome, best not to write incriminating things down.

Check.

Placing a fresh glass of water on the table before me, he sits back down and I am slightly impressed, and partly confused.

"You brought me water?"

"I brought you water," he confirms.

"Okay, so... is this you trying to woo me?"

"Damn it, Charmer, just drink the water and say thank you."

I do as he suggested, the cool water flowing down my throat and I lean back with a full belly, ready for some more answers.

"So we've been married for two years?"

"A little over that."

"A little," I parrot.

"Next question."

"What was on the note from the market?"

He stares at me as if gauging my reaction before he speaks.

"I can handle it," I lie, I have to know if he is willing to tell me the truth, because Noah already told me what the note said.

I have to know if he was serious about making this work,

building an *us*. If he lies to me, this is over, before it can really begin.

"*You won't get away from me this time*," he finally speaks, after what feels like an eternity. He leans forward, laying his arms on the table and sighing, "And there was another puzzle piece."

"What did it look like? Did it fit with the other piece?"

"We don't know yet if it fits, but it looked the same as the other, like a picture blown up and fuzzy."

I nod, chewing on the inside of my cheek.

Maybe instead of the 'why' I need to start focusing on the 'who'.

"Do you have any leads on who you think might be doing this?"

He runs a hand down his beard, and my heart sinks. I shouldn't have high hopes, the case has been cold for over two years. But, now we know whoever it is wants me to know something, and that they considered me theirs.

"I will exhaust every resource I have to find this piece of shit, Fern."

He stands up and leaves, and I'm left reeling by one simple fact. I'm stuck on it, because I didn't expect it.

Creed told me the truth.

Chapter Nineteen

After Creed left me on the back porch, I got up and went back into the house. I assume he went home, wherever the hell that is.

I snap my fingers, mentally making a note to ask him.

The doorbell rings, but I'm not there yet. I don't know who is on the other side of that door, and I'm not in the mood to play fake nice. Candy appears from the kitchen where a sweet smelling aroma wafts into the living room.

"Are you..." she trails off, noticing the way I press my body into the couch and sink further into my thoughts.

The lock clicks and it sends me back to that night, Gray's face as he held his throat, begging me to run.

The knife slashing through the air.

I take a deep breath, close my eyes, and try to focus, sitting there with memories replaying in my mind.

Black fabric covered almost every inch of the attacker, their eyes were zeroed in on me. My eyes pop open and I suck in a quick breath.

Their eyes, they were brown.

In the low light within the cabin of the SUV... they were brown!

Candy comes around the couch, scaring me from my thoughts.

"Whoa," she says, "Are you okay?"

I gulp and nod. I have to tell Creed, this has to help, right? I stand noticing the vase of peonies in Candy's hands. She has to hold the vase with two hands because it's full to the brim with cream flowers, just like from the market.

"I already checked the note," she smiles, "It's not creepy."

She places the vase in my hands and giggles a little as she walks back to the kitchen. Carefully I make my way up the stairs and back into my room, I need to change out of what I used for pajamas, and I am desperate to know what the note says.

Marty probably saw what happened and sent me new flowers.

I place them on my night stand and walk to my closet. No one asked me to do anything today, and I haven't seen Noah yet, so I dress casually. Jeans and a t-shirt with my boots.

They feel familiar on my feet, like I'm getting ready for a day on the farm. Even though they've been cleaned of all the dirt, mud, and horse shit that covered them when I arrived.

Heading to the bathroom, I brush my hair, it is naturally straight, so I never really use anything to style it. Before, Candy and I would go to the salon and get our hair done together. Highlights, lowlights, treatments, you name it.

I twirl a lock of my black hair around my finger, maybe we can do that again. It might help trigger another memory.

The flowers are mocking me now, partly because I'm a little scared, and another part feels nauseous thinking of who would have known that we had been to the market. Whoever this is, knows me well, or at least, the old me.

I pluck the card from between the butter soft petals.

To my surprise there is a handwritten card,

Since you dropped the others.
-Creed

And yes. Charmer... this is
me wooing you.

The smile on my face feels foreign, but I am giddy with excitement. He's trying, and maybe it's because he wants to, and not because he thinks he has to.

I sniff the flowers before placing my new phone in my back pocket. I figure if Noah wants to explore, I need to have it. The house is a bit louder now that everyone is awake. I make my way downstairs to the kitchen where mom and dad are at the small table, and Noah is heating up the leftover oatmeal I made.

"You look beautiful this morning, honey," my mother says, drawing attention to my presence.

"I feel better," I find myself saying honestly.

Noah smiles and my dad stands, coming to wrap his arms around me.

"Will you be okay with Noah today?"

"Of course," I tell him, leaning back to stare up at him.

"I've got to go into the office for a few meetings, and your mom is meeting the ladies for lunch," I poke my head around him to look at her.

I know it has only been two days, but it feels normal. Not like it used to be, but a new sense. Creed and I are on new terms, I am nowhere near ready to talk about how I feel or anything, but I can see that he is trying.

"And I need to run a few errands, check on the house, the bakery," Candy whispers.

"You opened a bakery?" I ask.

She smiles and nods, excitement in full on her face, "Yeah, would you want to come with me?"

"Are you kidding?" I practically skip to her, "That was your dream! Of course I want to go."

"Noah, is that okay with you?" Candy asks, and it doesn't register why until he answers.

"Of course, another good day will be good for you Fern, I need to make a few calls anyway."

"Will you tell Miss Loretta that I love her?"

He smiles, "You know I will."

Candy turns to me and lets out a squeal, "Let me get my keys!"

We ride in her car, which is much nicer than the one I remember. It isn't an SUV but it also isn't a small car. The seats are nice leather and she sings happily along to the bluetooth on the stereo.

Pulling up to main street, Candy takes one of the side streets and then an alley to park behind some conjoined buildings on this side of the road. She turns to me and smiles, throwing her arms around me.

"I'm so happy you're here."

"Me too."

I am, and I can see how much Manson loves her. The small things that the old me wouldn't have noticed. He takes every opportunity to touch her, even if it's just a passing brush. How he watches her to make sure she is okay.

"Do you love him?" I ask as we get out of the car.

Her features soften and silver lines her eyes, "I really do."

I believe her, she always had a thing for him, and I guess that night put things in perspective for her.

For them both.

It changed a lot of things.

She links her arm with mine and unlocks the metal door tucked away between the bricks. Inside the place is so bright, lit with fluorescents and there are a few people flitting about.

Silver tables take up the middle of the space, while huge industrial ovens line the wall to my right. Mixers with cages are on my left, along with rows of shelves on wheels.

"Whoa," I don't have any other words.

The place looks amazing, and I haven't even seen the actual bakery part for customers. A swinging door opens across from where I stand, taking it all in. A woman I recognize stands there, eyes bulging, and mouth open.

"Gretchen?"

"Well, if it isn't the queen bee of Gravity Hill," she crosses her arms over her chest, "I didn't think you would stay."

"Gretchen," Candy says, a clear warning in her voice.

"I didn't think you'd be working for Manson's wife either," I shrug, "But here we are."

Candy snorts beside me, and my eyes land on the younger

people in the room. A younger guy is kneading dough, flour covering his arms, and the apron he has on. Another young woman has a full piping bag thrown over her forearm swirling borders.

The last one however has his back to me, pulling out trays of what looked like croissants.

"Come on," Candy nudges me to a small office tucked behind one of the mixers.

It is small, painted bright yellow with a white desk and pictures of Candy and Manson. Pictures of their wedding, travels, even the bakery.

"I hate how much I missed."

Her chest rises and falls as she stops fiddling with the things from her bag. She pulls out a laptop and clicks the printer on.

"We eloped," she finally says, breaking the silence, "I couldn't have a wedding without you in it."

Our eyes connect, and I take the moment to really look at her. She is the same Candy that taught me how to kiss. The same person who would have done anything for me. She doesn't deserve to torture herself for something that happened so long ago, even if it is one of the most traumatic things to happen to me.

"I'm not mad at you, you know. Well," I pause and titter,

"I was, but I know it couldn't have been easy for you. I'm sorry you were the one who had to perform CPR on me in the bathroom."

Candy cries and comes around the desk to pull me into her arms.

"It wasn't your fault," she sobs, "I hated myself for a while, and Manson was in a really bad place. It took us months and a lot of therapy to really reconnect. Seeing you back here, it's like a time capsule, yeah we're older, but I still see my best friend."

"I shouldn't have gotten so upset when I got here. It wasn't fair of me."

She grips my shoulders and pushes me away so she can look me dead in the eyes, "Nothing about this whole shit show is fair, Manson and I are just happy you're here."

"Me too."

"Okay, let me do payroll, and then I'll show you the front!"

I nod and continue looking at the photos, feeling a twinge of sadness, I will never have a wedding. Won't get to walk down an aisle to my future husband and say vows. I will never get to hear how much someone loves me.

To know that they chose me.

I pull my phone out, deciding to finally check it. I have the time. It doesn't have a passcode, so that is the first thing I do, adding a code being easy enough. That's done quickly so I click on the contacts app.

There are so many, I don't remember having so many. It seems odd, but I continue, going to the photo app. It's mainly selfies of Candy and I. It makes me laugh and I make one my wallpaper.

Notification bubbles are on a few apps, but I start with the missed calls. Numbers I don't recognize are there, but nothing from that night. My family must have erased anything from then, hoping it would make things easier for me.

Since I know my number has changed, I wonder if my family programmed the new one into their phones. Silly of me to think they wouldn't, but I have to check.

"Hey, can I call your phone really quick?"

Candy nods and hands over her cell, still clacking away on her computer. Clicking on her contact on my phone I watch as my face flashes up on her screen.

She looks up at her phone in my hand, "Oh, I have your new number already, we all do."

"We all?"

"Your family, Noah, and Creed," she shrugs sheepishly and accepts the phone back.

I nod, that's probably for the best. The little red dot on

my messages app says three texts. The first is an unknown number asking for Gary, the second from Manson telling me to take it easy on Creed and to enjoy my "girls day".

I didn't even know he knew I was with Candy.

I should have known she would text him. It will be weird getting used to that. Candy and Manson communicating before her and I.

Hopefully one day Creed and I can be like that.

The last message is from Creed, my heart does a little jig in my chest. I open the message and have to bite my lip to stifle my grin. He asked if I got my flowers.

Typing out a quick, but short, response I click the screen off and pocket the cell.

Candy is folding checks into envelopes when I finally sit across from her.

"You're really knee deep in this, aren't you?"

She throws her head back and laughs, "Weird, right?"

"Super weird."

We laugh together, and I swear a chunk of my heart reattaches itself. Stitched back together by the warmth and forgiveness of my best friend.

She slaps her hands on her desk and pushes her rolly chair back, "You ready to see the front of the house?"

"Yes."

She leads me through the kitchen to the swinging door Gretchen came through. The front of the house–as she called it–is warm and colorful all at the same time. The windows are huge, covering the whole front, with swirling scripted writing and details.

"What did you call it?"

Her eyes hit the floor, "Fern and Flourished."

I swivel my head back to the window, they named their bakery after me? Racing out the door, I dodge a few people to get to the wooden doors with glass panes.

Outside, the display almost brings me to my knees, colorful swirls and desserts are the backdrop to a beautifully scripted 'Fern & Flourished'.

"You make our lives more colorful," she says, coming to stand beside me. "We love you, Fern."

I can see it then, the way the words are shaded in blacks and grays, how the colors behind it make the logo pop, and tell you exactly what they sell. But deeper, what only we can see is the love and hope for a friend and a sister to be okay. To defeat depression and anxiety.

I am shaking when I turn and vault into her arms.

"I love you too," I sob into my best friend's t-shirt.

She cries with me, and we stand there for a while, just soaking in all the feelings.

In that moment, I just know, I will be whole again.

Chapter Twenty

Candy and I wrap up at Fern and Flourished after eating our weight in sweets. She has the whole market cornered with her cookies alone. No wonder there aren't any other bakeries around.

She places paychecks in employee lockers and we leave after she locks the back door making me lift a brow in question.

"Manson and I agreed with everything going on not to let any of the employees use the back entrance, just in case," she looks away, and I know what she isn't saying. In case the murderer comes for someone in my family.

"I'm sorry y'all are having to worry about this at all."

"Don't, none of this is your doing," she stops before unlocking her car. "You know that, right?"

I knew that, but it still doesn't make the situation any easier. There is a stalker out there, and who knows what they are capable of?

"I know," I finally say. She seems happy with my response as she unlocks the doors and we slide in. She starts the car and we head to the house Manson built from her designs. I am so excited to see it, Candy has always been an incredible designer.

The drive isn't long, as with almost everything else in this town. Living on the ranch I had to get used to driving an hour just to get into town, here I can practically walk everywhere.

Their house is gated and I am grateful Manson thought of it. The iron gate swings open from the sensor on Candy's car, hidden somewhere I'm sure. When we pass through, the gate closes behind her car automatically.

"That's nice."

The driveway is long and paved in asphalt, with a circular drive in front. The house itself is grand, like I knew it would be, Manson never does anything half-assed. The two story house is long, stretching from one end of the circle drive to the other.

Columns a lot like our parents house hold the entire structure with a balcony in the middle. The board and batten is painted white, standing out against the green grass.

"It's beautiful," I almost smash my face against the window to keep looking, but restrain myself.

She snorts, "You should see yours."

Whipping my head in her direction, my brows kiss in the middle of my forehead, "Excuse me?"

She parks the car in an underground garage and unbuckles.

"Nothing."

"Oh no you don't," I struggle getting my seatbelt to release so I can follow her, but she is already at the door at the top of a small set of stairs.

Miming zipping her lips, she opens the door.

I'll drop it for now, because holy shit. Their house is gorgeous, marbled tiles line the floors, tan leather furniture sits in the living room, and the stairs sweep up the far left side of the house.

Everything is immaculate, surfaces clear of clutter, and polished to a shine. The kitchen and living room are open to the first floor, with a hallway to my left under the stairs, and another to my right.

"Candy..."

Everything is decorated in minimal taste. Silver and black with green accents. Nothing out of place, until Candy unceremoniously drops her bag on the counter, and I almost tell her not to disturb anything.

"Don't read too much into it," she laughs, "My closet is a mess."

We laugh, because if there is one thing about Candy that won't ever change, it's her inability to put clothes away.

"Come on," she pulls my arm in the direction of the stairs, "Manson's office is through there, along with the pantry."

We race up the stairs and she points out guest rooms, a game room, and then their bed room. I didn't notice the balcony that ran along the top of the living room.

It leads to double doors which turned out to be their bedroom. She opens the doors with a silly little bow and I step in.

The carpet is soft beneath my sock feet, I wouldn't dare wear my boots through such a clean house.

Their room is nothing like the rest of the house, this one is clearly lived in. Blankets are thrown over an unmade bed, and cords litter the nightstands. Three windows let in picturesque lighting. It makes me smile.

"Sorry it's messy, we don't let the cleaning crew in here."

I can understand that, they want something untouched by anyone other than them. Like their private sanctuary, and I don't want to intrude any further so I stop at the entrance. I appreciate that Candy wants to share her life with me, but I don't want to cross that line.

"It's perfect, Candy," she tilts her head at me quizzically and I smile, "but I'd rather not look at the bed you fuck my brother in more than once though."

She bursts into laughter, "Fair."

We head back down and Candy gathers a few things from Manson's office before we get back in the car. She drives to our old salon, and parks in the closest spot to the door.

"Surprise!"

I laugh and follow her out of the car and into the salon that holds so many memories. Candy walks straight back to Becca's station, by passing the receptionist who never even looks up from her phone.

"Well, well, well," Becca tisks, "If it isn't the dynamic duo, back again."

"Hello to you too Becca."

She rounds the chair to pull me in for a hug and I let her. Becca had been doing our hair for years before everything happened, and like any good beautician, she knows all of our secrets.

"Sit, sit," she says as she flourishes her hands, "You know the drill."

We do, sitting side by side in the black leather chairs. I swivel my chair to face Candy while Becca places the cape over her body and tightens the collar. They chat together as I look around.

Not much has changed, exposed ducts and beams are

painted black against the silver ceiling, and the wall with the shampoo bowls has been painted a light pink. The rest are made up of exposed brick. Mirrors hang from the ceiling by strong cables, and hair dryers are buzzing in the background.

It's pretty busy for a week day, something I probably wouldn't have noticed before. Almost all of the chairs are full, and the bright spotlights feel hot against my skin.

"Hannah is my assistant," Becca says, pulling me from my thoughts, "Do you mind if she does your treatment?"

Hannah is a cute pixie type, her shoulder length hair is dyed lavender and half done up in space buns. Her makeup is also dramatic, and it makes me smile.

"Hi, Hannah, I'm Fern," I introduce myself and she giggles.

"I know who you are," her voice is light, exactly what I imagined it would be. "You graduated a few years before me."

"Oh," I don't know what else to say.

Turns out I didn't need to say anything, Hannah is a motor mouth, telling me all of the town's gossip. I don't think she takes a breath until her hands land on my shoulders and her eyes go wide.

"What?" I look in the mirror, just to make sure my hair isn't falling out or anything. My eyes connect with sinful green ones and I spin the chair around.

"Shit, Creed," I stand, "I think you scared Hannah."

She's staring, eyes wide and mouth open, comb in one hand frozen halfway in the air.

"You haven't been answering your phone."

"And?"

"Well," he steps forward, bending down so we're eye level, "When I call my wife, I expect her to answer."

I close my eyes, why does he have to call me that? Yes, we agreed to try, but if the lawyer knew who he was, and with the way Hannah is staring at him, she knows exactly who he is too. That means everyone knows who *I* am.

Mrs. Hemlock

"I didn't hear it," I sigh.

He holds out his hand and I roll my eyes, digging into my back pocket to hand him the device and letting him do whatever he wants to it.

"Now you will," he leans down, wraps his arm around my hip and slides my phone back into my pocket. I inhale him, God why does he have to smell so good?

He kisses my cheek, turns around, and walks out, leaving me reeling. My skin is on fire where his lips touched my face. My whole body feels like one big inferno.

Someone clears their throat once the door closes behind

him, and I look around. My face has to be the color of a fucking firetruck. The whole salon was deathly quiet while they witnessed that spectacle, no white noise to be heard, and every single pair of eyes on me.

"Fuck me, " I murmur.

Candy laughs, loud and boisterous, "That's new."

I spin, shooting daggers at her with my eyes. I do not want to have this conversation with her and motormouth Hannah around.

She puts her hands up and laughs, spinning back around and shouting, "Nothing to see here!"

Slowly, everyone resumes going about what they had paused when Creed came in. Soon the salon is full of chatter once again.

My smoothing treatment has been applied and Candy's foils are in. We sit there, catching up and laughing. It's just what I need, after everything it was nice to come home and feel almost whole.

"Shit," Candy looks at her watch and pulls her phone from her purse, "I was supposed to drop those files for Manson."

"Where?"

"Across the street, his practice is on the second floor." She motions for Becca to remove her cape and briskly walks to the door.

I walk behind her, still in my cape.

"Are you sure that's a good idea?" I have a bad feeling about her walking across main street alone since the market incident.

"I'll be fine," she kisses my cheek and opens the door. "But you can watch to be safe."

I sigh, crossing my arms over my chest. I stand there, watching her every move. She looks left to right after grabbing everything she needs and takes off across Main Street.

Manson will get a kick out of her hair.

The minutes tick by as I wait, how long should it take? I mean, she said it was just on the second floor. These buildings are so old it probably doesn't have an elevator.

I take a beat, willing my head to rationalize the situation. Candy said she would be okay, and she will. I watch the minutes tick by on the clock, call her cell which rings inside the salon.

"I'm gonna go check on her," I tell the girl at the desk, but she just blinks and returns to her phone.

Okay.

I look both ways before crossing, the shop below is a cute little book store. It has a newly renovated smell to it mixed along with books.

A slim man pops around one of the shelves, scaring the shit out of me, "Hi! How can I help you?"

I rub my hand over my chest to ease the knot there, "I'm looking for Manson Hayes's office?"

"Oh," he chuckles, "The stairs are just there, behind the story time corner."

He points in that direction and I quickly thank him.

"I'm afraid he left though."

"Left?"

I look toward the stairs praying Candy is just chatting with someone and not hurt. Taking them two at a time I hit the top. There is a small waiting area and a desk, but no one is here. The lights are off, only a security lamp is on.

"Candy!" I shout, hoping she will call out laughing at my panicked tone.

There are three doors, immediately in front is a bathroom. The next is an office storage looking room, filing cabinets line the walls and a table sits in the middle.

The next door is harder to open, the knob turns easily enough, but it's heavy, or something is blocking the door. When I manage to get it open a crack, I find Candy's legs stretched out and in the way.

"CANDY!"

I howl, pushing harder on the door, blood streaks the

carpet as her body moves with the door. She fell directly in front of the door, as if she tried to get out. Her head has a goose egg and she isn't breathing.

"Fuck. Fuck. Fuck."

When I get the door open enough that I can slip through, I fall to my knees beside her and pull her further away from the door. She's cold, and pale, my shaky hands grapple for my phone. I press Creed's number, turn it to speaker, and let it ring as I assess her. She has red marks that bloom on her blouse, and when I pull the satin up I cry out for help.

Creed answers on the second ring, "Charmer?"

"Creed I need help!" I sob, "She's going to die!"

"What?" his voice is stern, and I can tell he is already in motion, "Where are you?"

"M-m-manson's office," I hiccup, "Candy said she forgot to drop off some files."

Coughing and sucking in tight breaths I struggle to get it out, my best friend is lying on the floor of her husband's office dying, because of me. "God, Creed. What do I do?" Snot pours down my nose and I wipe it away, "How do I-how do I save her? There's blood everywhere..."

"I need you to place your hands on the wounds, and apply pressure," he says, calm and steady as steel, "Charmer?"

"Ok-kay." I make sure the phone is still connected as I

place my hands on the wound that looks the worst, "There's so much blood."

"I'm on my way, Fern, don't let go of her."

I shake my head as her blood sticks to my hands, and sob, "why her?" I shout into the empty air. "Why," I whine and cough. I can't lose someone else.

I refuse to lose her, she's my family.

"Candy, stay with me, please," I beg, over and over I plead with her unconscious body to *stay*.

I don't know how long I sit here, screaming for help before I hear the sound of sirens nearing and see lights flashing in the windows. Police stomp up the stairs as I wail for them to come to me. They need to save her.

"I need a Rescue Ambulance here now," one of them says into their radio's mic.

"Ma'am," the other one bends low, "You did good, can you tell me her name?"

I lift my head to look at the officer, "Candy Hayes."

His eyes roam over her prone body and he starts chest compressions. How long can someone go without breathing?

"Keep your hands there," the officer tells me as he counts the pumps on her chest.

Emergency services come in and the police officer

transfers chest compressions to the EMT. He stands, coming around to my side and pulling me away.

"No!" I scream, scrambling back to her body to hold on to the wound like Creed told me.

"Fern?" I hear Creed's deep voice boom through the space, then I see him, filling the doorway with such force that I swear everyone stops for a moment.

I rise and run to him, unaware of the police officer's protests, and he wraps me up in his arms as I cry into his chest.

"I've got a pulse," one of the men in white says, "We need to get her on the stretcher."

Creed moves us while shouting directions about which hospital to take her to. I watch them load her up and carefully maneuver the gurney down the stairs.

"Manson," I bite my lips together to keep my sobs at bay.

"I told him where to go."

Creed never takes his hands off me, guiding me to sit on one of the couches in the waiting area.

"I need you to tell me exactly what happened."

Tears run in rivulets down my face, "But Candy…"

"Will be taken to the best hospital where the surgeon is already waiting."

He runs his hands up and down my arms while he kneels

before me. I want to go, I want to follow her there and make sure I never take my eyes off her again.

"Fern, I need you to talk to me," he reminds me softly, wiping his thumb across my cheek.

I tell him everything as a few more men come in and Creed barks orders at them too. They nod and get to work.

"What if she dies, Creed?"

"'*What if*' is not your friend." He stands, and I immediately feel the loss of warmth, "Stay here, and don't say a word to any of the cops."

I nod and watch as he speaks to the two guys who came in with him. One searches the bathroom and the file room, the other, Manson's office. My phone is ringing from the floor where I left it, but I can't bring myself to stand.

I cry and stare at the wall for what feels like hours, until Creed sits beside me, picking me up and bundling me into his lap. He rubs circles on my back and lets me cry and snot all over his button down.

"Boss."

Creed kisses my forehead and deposits me back on the couch, a blanket is thrown over me but I don't care. I'm too in my head, worried about Candy, fucking furious that they got to her. It should have been me, I should have been with her like I wanted.

I shouldn't have let her come alone.

God, I am so stupid.

This may have
only just begun,
But fear lies
within you now.
Terror is telling
you to run,
Though you
won't escape my
vow.
Be wary for all
those you love,
As no one is safe
from me.
I'll hunt you
down my little
dove,
I will make you
truly see.

Chapter Twenty-One

"Charmer, I need you to move," Creed murmurs in my ear, "We need to go to the hospital."

I turn over, eyes like sandpaper, "Is she dead?"

"Still in surgery. She lost a lot of blood."

He lifts the blanket and helps me up, placing the soft fabric around my shoulders. I didn't notice before, but Creed's clothes are bloody. Opening the blanket I look down at myself, it looks like I was the one who stabbed her.

Her blood has dried in the cracks and crevices of my hands, like tiny rivers on a map. It's under my nails, on my palms. I am going to need to scrub my hands so many times to get the image of them covered in my best friend's blood, out of my head.

One of the men with Creed hands him a wet paper towel, which he takes and nods them away. They clomp down the stairs, as Creed turns to me and begins wiping my face.

"She's going to be okay," he says while cradling my chin in

one hand while he cleans Candy's blood off my face. I must have smeared it when I was crying.

Our eyes are locked, and our breaths mingle.

"Promise?"

He nods, and it takes a little bit of the uneasy feeling away.

"Do you want to get cleaned up and then go to the hospital?" The way he asks what I want feels almost tender.

I remember I still have that treatment on my hair and I rush to the bathroom. Turning the sink wide open I frantically splash water on my locks. Washing my hair in a small sink is a task.

Creed's calloused hands join mine as he massages away whatever he can from the mask. I stand there, hunched over the sink, wringing my hair out and pause.

"It should have been me," I say into the sink, watching the water drain.

He doesn't speak, just uses the blanket as a towel and helps wrap it around my hair. He pulls me back into his chest and I melt into him, wrapping my arms around his waist, savoring the way his comfort feels.

Slowly we make our way out of Manson's bathroom to the stairs where the two men from before stand sentry. He nods to them and they move, it's odd to see, and my eyes keep bouncing back and forth.

We make the walk to Creed's blacked out SUV and he lifts me into the back seat while one of the guys slides into the other. Leaning over me, he clicks the buckle into place. His face inches from mine, but his expression is soft.

"Is it okay if Luca rides back here with you?"

I nod, and he leans in to place a kiss next to my lips. Quick, like a snake bite, he is closing the door and in the driver's seat. I pull my legs up on the bench using the middle as my personal foot rest.

Luca doesn't seem to care, and I turn to look out the window. Every so often tears escape my eyes as Creed makes the drive to Cardis Medical Center. It's about fifty minutes away from Gravity Hill, so I have plenty of time to get everything out before he puts the car in park at the front entrance.

Luca nudges my feet and gets out, leaving his door open so I can slide out behind him. I shake the blanket from my hair and leave it on the floorboard. Creed grips my hand as we walk in, and I don't think he knows exactly what he is doing, but it means everything to me.

Creed spots my mother first, her eyes red, and her cheeks puffy.

"Fern!" She cries out, "My God, Alexander she's here!"

My father comes around the corner of what I guess is the

waiting room. He rushes over to us and snatches me up in a hug so tight I am worried he might crack a rib.

"We thought," he swallows, "When Creed called, we thought the worst."

I shake my head and bite my lip to keep from crying. Manson emerges from a door to the left and runs to me.

My father lets me go and Manson scoops me up. His whole body trembles as he cries. It's my turn to do the holding, and I do, closing my arms around him and squeezing tight.

"She's going to make it," he says around quick breaths. "She'll be okay."

I lean back to look at his face, he's smiling and crying, a mix I haven't seen often.

"She's okay?"

He nods and we all hug him. Creed watches from a small distance away as our family let's relief and hope knit us together.

"When can we see her?"

"Will she need physical therapy?"

"Did she say what happened?"

"Whoa," Manson throws his hands up and we all pause. "She isn't awake yet, but the cops want to talk to her before anyone else."

Creed clears his throat and Manson nods. Stepping away from us, he goes to Creed and to my utter shock, they hug.

When they pull apart I watch them walk outside. Creed still hasn't told me what his people found, or if he did, I didn't hear him.

My parents and I sit on the plastic chairs of the visitors room. It's empty, other than dads security guy and the receptionist who looks none too thrilled to be here.

We don't speak, words are hard in a time like this. A limbo of sorts. I want to see her. To make sure she is whole and alive. I want to see the color in her cheeks like when Manson kissed her, or the sparkle in her eye when she thought she was being clever.

A doctor comes out of the door beside the receptionist desk, in mint green scrubs with a smile on his face.

"I assume you're Candy's family," he begins.

"Wait, let me get Manson."

I rush out of the room toward the glass doors. They swish as the sensor catches my movement.

Creed's head snaps up and he extends his hand, "What's wrong?"

"Nothing," I shake my head, "The doctor is here."

Manson looks from me to Creed and back. They both turn away from Luca and the other guy who I haven't officially met yet, and walk toward the doors.

Creed puts his hands on my neck and tips my head back, "Are you okay?"

Licking my lips, I decide to answer him honestly. I owe him that much.

I shake my head and bite my lip, "Not really."

He brings his forehead to mine, "What do you need?"

My chest is going to burst, my throat is closing, and my heart is working double time.

"I don't know," I whisper as a lone tear leaks out of the corner of my eye. He brushes it away with his thumb and smooths my hair behind my ear.

"Okay," he leans back and laces my fingers with his. Leading us back into the hospital.

The doctor is finishing up by the time we get back. Manson is smiling at every word and when the doctor finishes, Manson declares that he's going to see her.

With a kiss to my mother and I, he follows the doctor through the door.

"What did he say?"

My mother fills me in. Candy is awake and asking for Manson, she refused to speak to the police until he was there. Smart, even after surgery to save her life.

She will have to stay for another few days while her

wounds heal to make sure there is no infection.

"The doctor also said whoever found her, saved her life." I feel a rush of emotions, if it weren't for me she wouldn't even be here.

This psychopath has taken things too far.

"Creed helped me through it," I say, leaning into him for warmth.

"Speaking of," my father clears his throat, "I think it might be best if you stay with your husband tonight."

My eyes go round and I fight the urge to argue. I will have to move in eventually, we are married after all. It feels fast, but everything since I have gotten back seems that way, and Creed has been here every step.

"The house will be empty, and I don't think it's wise for you to be alone," he continues, as if my silence means I am thinking of an excuse.

"Okay."

Surprise registers on everyone's face, even Creed's for a split second.

"You take care of my girl," my mother warns him and I snicker.

He pinches my shoulder and I yelp.

"With my life," he swears, speaking to her, but staring at me.

I hug both of my parents and make them promise to call me the moment they see her.

We walk back to the doors where Luca has the SUV waiting and rumbling. Creed slides into the back after me and lifts my feet onto his lap.

I stare at him, slack jawed. Has he always been this...touchy?

"Seatbelt," he reprimands me.

It takes me a minute to process what he is saying, because he starts rubbing my feet and calves perfectly. If I could purr, I would.

He stops and tilts his head. Reaching behind me, I find the buckle and click it into place.

Luca drives decently through the streets and highways, his eyes hitting all the mirrors. I doze as Creed massages my legs and let the adrenaline wear off.

Chapter Twenty-Two

"**G**o get some rest," I hear Creed's voice. It's muffled, like there is a barrier between us. Panic floods my chest, and I shoot up, hitting my head on the armrest on my way up.

"Ow."

Creed opens the door, "Did we wake you?"

I shake my head, rubbing the spot that took the hit. He helps me out of the car and into what I assume to be another underground garage. It looks eerily similar to Manson and Candy's but with a few more bays.

"What's the other guy's name?" I should probably stop referring to him as *the guy with Luca* if he is going to be around.

"Nile, he's Diego's brother. Diego is my head of security," he speaks as he walks, and I follow. I don't want to be stuck down here while Luca and Nile do whatever it is they do.

"Okay."

"Why?" He throws a smirk over his shoulder.

"Because I should probably stop referring to him as 'the other guy' in my head."

He laughs, "The other guy works for me."

I roll my eyes but continue after him anyway. Creed types in a code near the door and a locking mechanism begins whirring as the gears click. The door in front of us pops open and he pushes it wide enough for us to go through.

We emerge through the door into a mudroom.

I must've missed something?

Does he plan on having a million children? There are cubbies upon cubbies, hooks drilled into the sage green wall, and a big area for what I assume to be dogs.

"Where are we? Summer camp?" I ask, still unsure where to look.

"This," he motions with one arm, "Is called a mudroom."

"No shit, how many people live here?"

He shrugs, "I wanted to make sure we had enough space."

"For a whole football team?"

He laughs and hooks his arm around my waist, "We have time."

I push him away and take my shoes off, placing them in a cubby and walking through an arch. It is a short hallway, a chestnut door with mesh in the center sits to the left, and when I peer inside I notice vegetables and canned food.

"A pantry well stocked?" I smile a cheeky smile and continue.

The kitchen... holy fucking *shit*, the kitchen is huge. Cabinets line a whole wall, and the island can easily seat ten.

"Who are you feeding? An army?"

He chuckles, "Not quite."

"Creed, this place is huge," I take in the state of the art appliances and crisp clean white cabinets. The countertops are a gorgeous marble, with gray and black veins.

I'm actually scared to look in the dining room, fearing that he had a custom table made to accommodate thirty people. So I pretend not to see it and continue on my merry way to the living room where I can hear voices. There are men on the couches, video game controllers in hand clicking buttons as fast as they can, jumping up and screaming at one another.

I look back at Creed with a raised brow.

"Boys," Creed yells, "Knock it off, there's someone I want you to meet."

The boys all put the controllers down and gather at the bottom of what I now realize is a sunken living room.

"This is Fern," he says, placing his hands on my shoulders, "My wife."

The way he says wife sends shivers up my spine, and the boys all make noises and holler. They can't be any older than eighteen.

"Alright, alright," he steers me around the living room to the floor to ceiling windows. They're stunning, and I imagine when the sun rises the lighting in here will be magnificent.

I can see a huge pool and sun deck with chairs littered about.

"Do you want me to turn on the lights?"

He whispers in my ear, sending goosebumps along my skin. I nod, even though I am exhausted from today's events. On his phone he taps a few buttons, and slowly lights start to blink on. Bulbs of warm yellow light cast a soft glow onto the patio, and I can see myself sitting out here and enjoying the peace.

"Do you like it?"

"Yeah," I smile and turn to face him, "It's my dream house."

He smiles down at me and I almost swoon, or maybe that's the lack of sleep I've been feeling.

"Let's get you cleaned up and ready for bed."

We wave goodnight to the boys who fired up their video games once again and are hooting and hollering louder than before. My mind conjures up reasons why they're all here, did they not have homes to go to? Parents?

"Don't worry, we can't hear them on our side of the house."

I let him take my hand and lead me up the stairs, focusing on the part of his statement about our *side*. At the landing he takes a right, down a long hallway with very few doors.

The last door, directly in front of us, is locked with another key pad. Creed types in a code and the same tinkering noises come from the wall like with the garage door.

"No one is allowed in here," he lets go of my hand and pushes the door open, "Until you."

It is an amazing space. Couches sit in the middle of the room, separated by colorful rugs and a table. All black Victorian furniture, nothing vintage here, all of this is new. I can smell the oils from the leather polish.

"This is your room?"

I can't help my curiosity about him. This is his space, and I've never seen it before. There is a bar to the left of the sitting area stocked with crystal decanters full of different hued liquids.

"Our room," he corrects, "When you're ready."

Standing here in the doorway of an impossibly gorgeous house, with an incredibly beautiful man I can't help but compare. I have never been insecure about my body, or the way I look, but I never had the scars I have now. I've never had the threat of death always lingering, and I don't want him to be the trigger. He was the one who listened to me, saved me, how can I *not* connect him to that night?

Instead of speaking, I walk into the room. Through an arched passage leading to the bedroom. The bed has to have been custom made, it looks huge, or maybe it's the room. Vaulted ceilings are hand painted to look like venetian tiles, the walls are a light green, almost the color of Creed's eyes.

The bed matches the Victorian chairs, black on black with carved legs. It's a dream bed, not something that could possibly exist.

"You're keeping me in suspense, Charmer."

I almost forgot he was there, this can't be real.

"It is very real," he assures me.

I guess that last part wasn't just in my head.

"The bathroom is to the left, and to the right is the closet. Do you want to get cleaned up?"

I nod, needing to get out of the clothes covered in my best friend's blood. I can smell the hospital as if it clings to every fiber.

He walks to the left and I follow. I shouldn't be surprised, but alas, here I am. The bathroom boasts a large garden tub in the center with a rainfall faucet hanging over it.

A walk in shower that could easily fit ten people is to the left, and the double sinks within the vanity are to the right. Products line the shelves in neat rows, brand new makeup, all of my favorites, sitting on the vanity.

My eyes catch his in the mirror and he whispers, "It's always been for you."

"The house?"

He snorts and shakes his head.

"Everything, Charmer. You think you aren't under my skin, in the memory of my muscles, the marrow of my very bones?"

I'm completely shell shocked. Is he admitting he *already* loves me? Or that he always has? His strides are powerful as he walks up to me. I spin around so I can watch his face, he's dropped the hard exterior, letting me see who he is underneath all the bravado.

Who I've always known him to be, before everything happened and I lost years to depression, and fear.

"Then you haven't been paying attention."

His mouth slants over mine, and I let out a noise I have never made before. Creed is kissing me so gently my knees threaten to give out. His lips move over mine, coaxing me to open, and I do. I let him sweep his tongue out to meet mine as one of his hands grips the back of my neck, cupping my face, and the other lands on my hip.

He pulls away too soon, if this is all I'm going to get before he changes his mind, I want to savor it. Gripping my fists into his shirt I pull him back in, pressing my soft body into his hard one.

I want him. *Fuck*. I want everything he is willing to give me.

We break apart, breaths heavy, chests heaving.

"My skin comes alive when you're near me, Charmer. It always has, you're like a fucking lighthouse to my turbulent seas," he swallows, "And if you'll have me, I'd like to marry you."

I search his eyes. I am so gone for this man, always have been, and at this moment, even though I've only been back for three days, and my best friend is in the hospital, all I want is him.

"We're already married," I point out in a whisper.

"I mean, if you want a wedding," he takes my hand in his, and his finger circles where a ring would sit, "I'll give you everything I have, Fern, with everything I have."

"Why now?" tears escape as reality crashes down around us. "When the people around me are dying, and being hunted like deer."

His hands slide around my neck, fingers tangling in the

hair behind my ears.

"When I found you that night," he exhales a long breath. "Everything changed. Before, I had to stop myself every time I wanted to touch you. I couldn't let myself fall for the girl that made my dull colors brighter, because of who I am, because of what I've done. But that night...that night I said fuck my family and I broke all the rules, for you."

"What rules?" I don't understand. I've wanted him for years, but couldn't have him because *he* wasn't interested, or so I thought.

"My father has basically planned my whole life. Everyone was sure he would choose me to take over everything, to be his second," he closes his eyes, as if remembering, "Saving you, was not part of his plan, and it...split hairs."

"When Manson found you in your bathroom half dead, I knew I had to make a drastic change," he leans back to watch me as I hang on his every word, "I should let you clean up, it's late, and I'm sure you would rather rest."

He stands up and turns but I grab his arm, "Wait, I want to hear this."

"It's not a pretty story, Charmer."

"I don't care," I step into him, missing the contact we just started to explore, "I feel like everything is changing, rapidly and I can't catch up."

He kneads the back of his neck and it hits me that maybe *he* needs the rest he's trying to offer me. He has to be busy, and I still need to tell him what I witnessed today.

"How about this," I offer, choosing to be bold and channel my inner Fern, the one who shattered, but was rebuilt, "Let's take a bath, I'll tell you everything I remember from today and we'll go to bed."

"Charmer," he releases a breath. "We don't have to."

"I'm pretty sure from your speech that you more than like me, and I *know* I more than like you. We can share a bathtub, especially one as big as that one."

I can tell he's thinking about it, he just needs a push, and I know exactly which buttons to press.

Slowly, I peel off my shirt, revealing my scars and stretch marks. My chest flushes when I find his eyes devouring my body, and I'm not even naked yet.

He rumbles, bringing his fist to his mouth and biting his inked knuckle.

I don't stop, and he doesn't leave as I loop my thumbs into my jeans and tug them down my legs. Pulling them off with my socks, I am left in a bra and thong that don't match. My bra is plain, a black cotton thing that affords me comfort, and lift.

"I should leave," he whispers. "Because I've wanted you

for too long, Fern."

When my eyes catch his I unhook my bra and let it fall to the floor between us. The air feels thick with anticipation and hope, as his eyes drink me in, and his hands twitch by his sides.

"Prove it," I dare him.

"I don't trust myself with you," he grunts out as I sway toward him.

I need him to erase every other person who has shared pleasure with me. I need to do something I want, something that will make me forget about this stalking murderer.

I need *him*.

"Be careful, Charmer," he warns, "With tits like those, any man would gladly go to his knees for you."

"I don't want just any man," I lean against him on my tippy toes and kiss him, just a soft brush of my lips against his, "I want you."

He grips my ass and hauls me up and against him, kissing me with abandon. He moves expertly through the bathroom, stepping over my clothes and setting me on the sinks. I fist his shirt, pulling on either side to pull it out of his slacks.

With quick movements he unbuttons and shrugs out of his shirt not even breaking the kiss when he undoes his belt and slings it across the room. Running my hands over the dips and ridges of his stomach I groan as the muscles there contract and move under his skin.

His hands go to my breasts and his eyes roll back as he kneads them, rubbing my nipples into stiff peaks.

"Tell me to stop," he begs.

"Not a chance in hell."

I palm him through his black pants, feeling how fucking hard he is for me. It will take some work to seat him fully inside me, but fuck if I'm not up for the challenge.

"It's been a while," he chokes out as I stroke him.

"Me too," I nip his beard and he catches my lips with his as he goes to his knees before me. Kissing me and slipping his fingers under the band of my thong, he pulls it down in back and forth motions until they are off and I am completely naked for him.

"I'm going to eat you alive, Charmer," he threatens and my skin is on fucking fire. I have no doubt he will make good on that promise, and I want to see him unravel for me. Lifting one leg, I plant my foot on the counter, opening myself up for him.

"Fuck me," he rumbles, deep and feral.

I do the same thing with the other leg and goddamn, he doesn't disappoint. His eyes zero in on my dripping pussy, and he groans before licking a featherlight trail over my clit. Shivers run over my body, and my muscles threaten to lock up as I moan.

"Shit," I breathe out, leaning my head back on the mirror.

He slaps my cunt and I jump in alarm. It's a sharp pain that lasts no more than two seconds, but it gets my attention.

"You watch me while I feast like a fucking king on your pretty little pussy."

It's my turn to say *fuck me* as he dives in, licking my skin like it's his favorite ice cream and I am the last of it. He buries his face between my legs, assaulting my clit with his expert tongue. I wiggle my hips, hoping to hold off my orgasm, because he is beyond good at this.

Quick as a snake striking he slaps my cunt again, ripping a moan from low in my throat.

"Don't you dare deny me what's mine," his voice is gravely and has me almost begging for more. "You cum on my face like the greedy fucking whore I know you are."

I gasp as his palm cracks across my pussy once more and he says, "Scream for me, baby."

He shoves a finger inside me and laps at my clit. With his other hand he pinches my nipple, and I lose my grip on reality.

I shatter into a million fragments, shaking, tightening, and whimpering. Heat races to my cunt as he pulls every last tremor from my body. My back arches, shoulders pressing into the mirror, I run my fingers through the long waves of his hair as he pushes another finger in and curls them like a fucking master.

"Again, Fern," he ghosts across my lips. I can smell my release on his lips, see the pleasure he wrung from my body in his beard.

I am a panting mess, struggling against his fingers. The sounds they make heighten my arousal, and when he sucks one of my nipples in his mouth I crumble all over again to the symphony of his fingers suctioning and releasing in my pussy,

Screaming out his name over and over again as I soak his hand and cry out in ecstasy, he growls, *"Good fucking girl."*

I am completely spent and high on endorphins as he leans over to fill the tub, pants slung low on his hips. He isn't real, I have to be hallucinating. Two orgasms in less than ten minutes can't be *real*, it has never happened.

He glances over his shoulder and smirks, dumping a bottle of something that looks suspiciously like bubbles and smells like a freshly peeled orange, into the tub.

He lifts back up to me, and I let my legs wrap lazily around his hips, locking him in.

"I don't know if I can top that," I admit, "But I'm willing to find out."

Lifting my chin with a finger and chuckling he says, "I've waited years to have you in my bed, I can wait another few days."

"Days?" I don't want to stop. I have him—all of him—in this room, and I'm not ready for it to be over.

He wraps his arms around my body and lifts me off the counter, carrying me to the tub and gently lowering me into the warm water.

"You aren't ready for that tonight."

My face betrays my feelings because he snatches my chin before I can look away in embarrassment.

"I wasn't kidding when I said that I'm all yours," he stares at me as if he can compel his way into my brain and etch the words there. "You are my world, baby. I went against our whole family when I chose you, I swear nothing will change when we walk out those doors."

A few tears trickle down my cheeks. I needed to *hear* everything he just said despite knowing it deep down, and my heart lets go of a weight I felt but could never shake.

"I waited for the right time, for the possibility that Manson wouldn't kill me for wanting you," he smears the tears on my cheeks with his thumbs, "And when I had to send you away,

I knew I was done waiting for the pieces to fall into place."

He kneels by the tub, gently running his hand over my hair.

"How did you know I would come back?" I wasn't even sure myself, whether I wanted to. The only reason I did was because Noah and Miss Loretta told me it would be temporary, that I could go back to the farm.

"I told you, I made a plan." He remarks, twisting his hair up and tying it with a band.

"The plan that isn't a pretty story," I nod, looking down at the water.

"I'll tell you everything, I swear it," he runs his idle fingers over my back as he speaks. "But you've been through so much in the last seventy-two hours, I want to make sure you're okay."

"It was an accident," I hiccup around the words, "I didn't mean to take that many pills... or maybe I did. Some things are still foggy in my head, I haven't been able to recover those memories," which may be a good thing.

"How about you let me take care of you, tonight," he stands, grabbing a washcloth and the shampoo I like, "We can talk about all of this in the morning."

I agree, but only if he gets in the tub with me. I can tell he wants to say no, that he is still seeing me as this fragile doll to look after.

"Please," I murmur, watching his face as he shuts his eyes and lets out a defeated sigh.

"I don't want to hurt you," he tentatively pushes his slacks down to his ankles, pulling them off along with his socks, everything he wears is black right down to his boxer briefs.

"I can handle a little pain."

He scoffs with a smile and lowers the black material of his boxers. I want to do a great many things to him, but I reign it in and resist. I have a feeling if I push him too far he'll pull back. His cock is exactly what I envisioned all these years.

Standing proud and thick, not too long, but definitely above average. I want to lick the veins that run the length of him, mapping them with my mouth. I want to know what drives him wild, what makes him tick.

He blushes under my blatant perusal, and I want to kick my legs in glee. He shifts, lifting a leg into the tub and lowering it into the water, following it up with the other. We are facing each other now, and I giggle.

Maybe I did need rest, because I can't help it. The way it bursts out of my chest and echoes in the room.

"You just fucked me with your mouth, made me cum twice and squirt all over your fingers, but you wont hold me in the tub?" My hysterics continue, there is something seriously wrong with me.

He grips my ankles under the water, pulling me toward him and wrapping my legs around his hips. His legs straighten out, and water splashes over the rim of the tub.

"Better?" He asks against the skin of my neck.

I nod, folding my arms around his neck and laying my head between his shoulder and neck. The water makes a line at my chin, but I don't care. Everything I've ever wanted is sitting in this tub with me, and he made me promises.

Promises that I will hold him to, till death.

"You never gave me an answer," he remarks into the silence. "About marrying me."

We've been sitting here long enough for the water to turn cold, and our skin to wrinkle but neither of us is ready to let go.

I lean back, sitting up and locking eyes with him, "well, I haven't sampled the dick yet," I tease and he tickles my sides. I thrash in the water and yelp.

"Okay, okay!" My voice rises higher and higher. When he finally lets me go, I pull his face to mine, my hands on either side of his cheeks and kiss him. Slowly, without any rush, because I am so in love with this man, and if my words can't say it, my body can.

His hands press into my back as he molds us together, "I'll

take that as a yes."

I nod vigorously, our noses brushing against each other. He twists a knob on the outside of the tub letting the cool water drain out until he can refresh it with hot water.

"Turn around and let me wash your hair."

My treatment earlier was interrupted, so the only rational choice is to let him do it. God only knows what it looks like. I turn, careful not to wiggle too much on his cock and make him grumble about *trying to wait* and *being a gentleman*.

When my ass hits the bottom of the tub he pulls an attachment from the side. I lean over, trying to see where all this stuff is coming from.

"It's like a magic Marry Poppins bag back there!"

He chuckles and directs me to tip my head back, the detachable sprayer was at the perfect setting, not too harsh, but also not dripping. He hangs the sprayer over the edge and lathers my hair in the shampoo I have always favored.

"Did you raid my bathroom?"

He snorts, "No, I took pictures and had one of the boys go get what you liked."

I twist around, with a quizzical look, "One of those boys, downstairs?"

"Yes, Charmer," he states, turning me back around so he can continue massaging the shampoo into the strands. "So they live here? And they'll get me whatever I want?" I ask, biting my lip.

He pauses his ministrations, "Within reason."

"Well, what's your definition of reason?"

He starts the sprayer back up, rinsing the shampoo out of my hair. He grabs the washcloth and dunks it under the water before soaping it up with a peppermint soap I found at the market.

"Mmmm," my eyes flutter, the smell alone is fantastic, and the way it leaves my skin hydrated is a huge bonus. Plus, shop local and all.

"If you need something just ask, Charmer, and it's yours."

"That's a dangerous power to give me," I warn. "What if I ask for a helicopter, or a pet jaguar?"

"We have a helicopter," he swiftly answers. "And why the fuck would you ask for a jaguar?"

"You're a mob boss, don't you need a mascot?"

"Oookay," he laughs, "Time for bed."

He helps me stand and washes off the remaining residue of the soap. When I am finally bubble free, he bundles me up in a towel and ties one around his waist.

Running the towel over my body he makes sure every inch of me is dry and leads me to the closet, where he slips me into one of his undershirts, and hands me a pair of leggings.

I didn't realize how tired I was until he pointed it out. My eyes are heavy with fatigue and I feel like I could sleep for days.

"I don't sleep in clothes," I whine.

"You had them on when I came to check on you the other night."

"Because Noah was in my room, and he probably wouldn't appreciate the view," I tell him, "He wouldn't sleep with me."

The muscles in Creed's face clench and I see him holding back his tongue, "I'm going to tell you this once, okay Charmer? I never want to hear you say another man's name, and anything sexual in the same sentence again."

"Oooooh," I giggle, letting them run rampant out of my mouth, "so he *is* jealous."

"I'm a jealous fucking bastard, baby, and I don't play fair."

I kiss him, because I can, because he's mine, and God it feels good to just do what I want. Creed gives up on trying to clothe me in more than his shirt, and tucks me into bed, promising to return after he showers. I nod, already half-way asleep between the green satin sheets.

The water turns off quickly, as if he knows I am falling asleep and wants to be in the bed with me. Decked in just his boxers he slides into the bed with me, his arms scooping me up and pulling me into his chest.

He is so warm, solid, and I feel the safest I have in a long time.

Years.

Sleep pulls me under swiftly and I relax completely into his embrace.

Chapter Twenty-Three

Waking up is hard, I'm all warm and bundled up in solid arms. My eyes are heavy as I blink them open.

"Good morning," Creed rumbles and kisses my temple. "How are you feeling?"

"Warm."

I stretch my arms up, feeling my muscles contract and pull.

He chuckles and rolls us so he has a leg pressed between mine, pinning me to the bed under his weight. It is an absolutely delicious way to wake up. I can feel the hardness of him against my leg, and it only makes me want to stay here.

"How did you sleep?"

"Perfectly," and I had. No nightmares, no cold sweats. It is the best sleep I've had in a long time.

"Good, because you won't be sleeping anywhere else from now on."

I suppress a smile and raise a brow, "And what if I refuse?"

"I'll have to chain you to my bed."

I can't tell if he's joking, his face is serious, but the way he says it makes my pulse pound and my heart hammer in my chest.

"I might like that."

He groans, rolling back over and covering his face with his arm, "You're going to be the death of me."

"What a sweet death that would be," I laugh, rolling out of bed and heading to the bathroom.

I relieve myself and wash my hands before heading back to the bedroom. Creed is gone, so I check the closet and find him half dressed in slacks, looping his belt through the loops.

Leaning against the door frame I cross my arms over my chest. I am oddly comfortable standing naked before him.

"Not that I'm complaining," he says, slipping his button down over his arms, "But I did have your clothes brought over this morning."

"The boys?" I guess.

He nods, "Everything is in the sitting room, but I can have one of the cleaners unpack it for you."

I eyed him, still appreciating the view, but suspiciously now.

"What?" He stops buttoning his shirt two buttons from the top and gives me his full attention.

"You haven't asked me about what happened with Candy at Manson's office," I pause giving him the chance to answer before the but, except he just stands there with his eyes roving over my body. "But, last night you told me you wanted the story before we…"

I don't quite know what to call last night, a declaration of love? Even though neither of us said the words, I feel it, and I know he feels it. Plus a fan-fucking-tastic display of his oral capabilities, definitely didn't hurt. Though, he probably won't appreciate the genius of my brain this morning.

"Desecrated our bathroom?"

"Well, I'd say more like christened," I look to the side, "Hmm, I guess what we did wasn't very biblical…desecrated it is!"

His lips turn up into a rare smile. Sure he's smirked in the past, but this isn't like that. This smile moves his beard and cheeks, making his eyes smaller and his cheeks pinker.

"Can you get dressed?" He asks, "Because if you don't we won't be leaving."

I roll my eyes, but turn around to head to the room before the bedroom, jiggling my ass and earning a groan from him.

He wasn't kidding, all of my shit was packed into the room.

Clothes are still on hangers laid neatly over the couches, shoes lined up in rows, just like I'd had them in my closet. Bras, underwear, and yoga pants had been thrown in bags. I had a feeling Creed threatened to castrate the boys if they looked at my underthings.

I don't know where we are going, but that doesn't really matter. I dress for my mood, not for the destination. Shuffling through the things on hangers, I find the dress I've been looking for.

It's a floor length black cotton dress with sleeves that go to my elbows. A band stretches around my torso under where my bra sits, and the rest flows down my legs. It is simple, and comfortable. I have to step around the bags of underthings to get to the vans I want to wear.

Pulling socks out of the bag of unmentionables is how Creed finds me, and he laughs, "Having trouble?"

My socks are mismatched, but do their job all the same. I hold them up and smirk, "Nope."

He shakes his head as I lace up the dark plum vans I chose and hop up to head for the door. He meets me there, opening the door for me to step out first. I hear the lock click into place and spin around, face planting into his chest.

I look up at him, "What's the code to the door?"

If it's going to be 'our' room I need to be able to access it, and he never said anything about a code.

"There's a scanner under the keypad," he steps back so I can see. "Put any of your fingers here," he hooks his middle finger under the buttons and I have to bend down to verify he isn't fucking with me.

He chuckles and the locking system whirs and clicks, "And you're in. No code."

"So the keypad is a decoy?"

He boops my nose with the same finger he used to open the door, "Now she's getting it."

I swat his hand and scoff, I'm not stupid. Well, maybe I am a bit sheltered, but not stupid.

"Come on," he places his hand on my lower back and delicious heat zips up my spine.

I follow him down the hallway to the stairs where I can hear more boy conversations. They are loud and bickering, it is very entertaining to watch.

"Do they live here?"

He stops on the last stair to watch them, "Yeah."

"Why?"

It's not that the house isn't big enough, or that I don't want them here. I just want to understand, they aren't his kids, so why are the four boys here?

"Their fathers and I are like brothers, Nile, Diego, Luca,

they all stood with me when I made my plan," he looks at me then, his face solemn, "I couldn't have done what I did without them. I wouldn't have *you* without them."

"What did you have to do?" I ask for the second time.

He sighs and I know he is about to tell me again that it was a messy story, but instead he tells the boys not to kill each other until we get back and hauls me to the car.

"I planned to do this a different way," his eyes slide my way for a second before he focuses back on the road, "However, my wife is impatient."

He isn't wrong, I am.

But if we are ever going to make it long term, I have to know everything. I have to know who he is, even if it isn't something I like. Even if it isn't pretty, and wrapped in a bow. Even presents can be shit inside.

We drive in silence for the rest of the ride. I can almost see the trepidation in his body language as he parks his car and turns to face me.

"I won't lie to you, I've done a lot of things that aren't ethical, morals have no place where the mob is concerned."

Nodding, I give him the space to say what he needs to.

"That's changing," he sighs, "Slowly, but it's already in motion. We have to do some of the more unsavory things to move pieces on the board."

"Okay," I'm officially confused, we're parked on the side of a dirt road about an hour out of town, and he is talking about chess?

"If we go down this road, there is no going back," he pauses and looks away.

I reach over the console and lay my hand on his cheek, turning him to face me, "I've waited for the pieces too."

Then I kiss him, I can't go back after last night, nothing short of death will pull me from him. His lips move over mine and when we part he closes his eyes and leans his forehead against mine.

"I love you, Fern."

My eyes snap up to his, my heart beating fast, trying to pound its way out of my ribs. My stomach hits my throat and I forget how to breathe.

I collide into him, climbing over the console and grabbing the sides of his face so he has no choice but to look into my eyes, "I don't give a damn what you've done before, because I love you Creed Hemlock. I have for a long time."

His hands are on my hips and he crushes his lips into mine while I pour everything I have into this kiss. His hands run over my sides and into my hair, where they curl and pull the strands.

"I've waited a lifetime to hear you say those three words

to me," his breath mingles with mine as our bodies shift with exhalations.

We sit there for a beat, kissing and soaking up the moment.

He pops open the door and helps me out, untangling my body from his lap. He steps aside and shuts the door, grasping my hand as he starts down a worn dirt path I hadn't noticed.

We walk for a few minutes, until the hill turns into a grassy meadow. Fresh dirt looking like it has been tilled in a few piles on the edges of the wild flowers.

"My mother was a saint," he tells me, grabbing my hands and pulling me down to sit in his lap. "She moved me here when she found out that my father sold my future to the Romero family. He let her, on the condition that I be sent to him a few weeks out of each summer."

"Manson and I hit it off the first day we met, and I couldn't be more thankful for him. But I haven't been able to be honest with him about a lot of my life. To keep him safe, I've had to lie to him, I won't do that with you." He looks at the flowers with a serene and anguished expression, and it's a few moments before he resumes his story.

"This is where my mother is buried, it's the only thing she requested after she got sick."

I remember those years, Manson spent more time at Creed's house than at home. He would come home crying some nights, even though he tried to hide it.

"I come here when I need to think, or get away. It makes me think of her and what she would do."

Sitting with my back against his chest I can't see him, but I can feel the amount of weight he has been carrying.

"After she died, I told my father that I wouldn't be used as a pawn in his empire, married off to the highest bidder. That I already had someone I loved," he squeezes me tighter to his chest. "My brother backed me up, it was the first time he had gone against anything my father planned. After we said our peace, my father called in our allies. He told them about the marriage, and that it would be dissolved. Over half of the families agreed."

"A few were upset, but ultimately the Romero family didn't bring enough to the table for me to sacrifice my heart. The Romero family was outraged. They are a small operation, and had been wanting an in with our family for decades."

"Bridgett found out about our marriage contract being forfeited. The Jane Doe in the woods? It was her, she followed you that night, sent me pictures of you and Gray."

The flash that night, it wasn't the knife. It was someone

taking pictures of us. I squirm, feeling violated, "How did she know who I was?"

"A few of the families that were once loyal to us, helped her find you. She was pissed, not thinking straight, and it got her killed. Whoever was chasing you in the woods must have found her first."

"I called my brother after they admitted you into the hospital. I thought whoever killed Gray and attacked you must be related to the Romero's. That night I flew to my brother, and together we captured and interrogated Bridgett's dad."

He sighs, his chest rising high and falling back down, "We tortured him, for days, until he admitted to sending someone after you. By then it was too late, Manson had found you in your bathroom, blue and non-responsive."

"I put a bullet in Romero's brain, and then my brother and I went after the rest of the men who betrayed us."

It's a lot to take in, and I can tell it takes Creed more effort that he will admit to tell me this. As if he's afraid that killing someone that wanted to hurt me—that did hurt me—is something I can't handle.

I turn in his lap, facing him so he can see just how sincere my words are, "Good fucking riddance."

He closes his eyes and snickers, "Only you could forgive

a monster like me."

"You're not a monster for protecting the people you love."

"I killed twenty four people that night."

"They betrayed your family, they almost killed me. Would they have stopped at me?"

"I don't know," he shakes his head and opens his eyes. "But I do know that before, they wouldn't let me choose you, and deep down I knew it would always have ended that way, because I can't live in a world where you don't exist."

"I'm sorry you've had to carry that alone," I whisper, tugging him in by his neck to press my lips against his. "How did you get the police not to identify Bridgett's body?"

"Throw a little money around, and things can disappear."

"That's not scary at all," I snort.

"It's reality in my world."

"Our world."

We stay like that, with me curled in his lap, listening to the birds sing their songs. I'm not going to rush him, he is giving me the pieces to his life, and I am happy to gobble them down.

Whenever he is ready to tell me everything, I'll be right by his side.

Chapter Twenty-Four

When we leave the meadow he drives me to the hospital where Candy is recovering. Manson is sitting beside her bed, head on his arm, sleeping. Candy is sitting up, stroking her fingers through his messy hair, eyes closed.

They look so peaceful.

"Maybe we should come back," I whisper, trying to be as quiet as possible.

Candy's eyes pop open and she smiles, she doesn't move much, I assume stitches are a bitch to move in.

"You're okay," she croaks.

Tears line my eyes and I rush to her other side, "Me?!" I almost shriek. "You were stabbed."

"I'm okay," she attempts a shrug but only winces.

"I thought I lost you," I tell her, tears streaking down my face as I grip her hand.

"But you didn't," she shifts, waking Manson in the process.

We all look at one another, I don't know what they are feeling, but I'm relieved we're all here, alive.

"Candy," Creed begins, "Can you tell us what happened?"

She nods, and I stop her, "Wait, if you aren't ready to talk about it, we can wait."

"We really can't," Manson argues, "This stalker is getting out of hand, they almost killed her, who's to say they won't come back?"

I wish I could say no one, but that would be a lie, and I won't lie to anyone in this room. Ever again.

"I walked into Manson's office," Candy takes a deep breath, "The lamp was on, but your office was shut. I didn't think anything of it, until I opened the door and found a man standing behind his desk."

"I turned around, ready to sprint to the book store and get help. But he grabbed my hair and the foils slipped out. I took off but he was faster, he tackled me to the ground and I hit my head. I was panicked and face down. He got up and pulled me back into your office," she is looking at Manson and my heart breaks for her. "He told me to stay quiet, but I was already screaming, I couldn't stop. It's like my brain just shut off."

"We sound-proofed the office, for privacy," Manson shakes his head, "I'm so sorry, baby."

"He got mad and started throwing this knife around, he was talking to himself, muttering something. He turned around and that's when I stood up and tried getting out the door." She cries silent tears that trickle down her cheeks.

"He locked it, and I must have made too much noise because he grabbed my arm and threw me back down. That was when he stabbed me. It hurt and pain was the only thing I could feel. The doctor said I went into shock, but I remembered him raising his arm and stabbing me two more times. I screamed, I know I did. But no one came."

My best friend is strong as fuck, talking about her attack like she wasn't the one who lived it. Like she is on autopilot.

"The last thing I remember was him leaving."

We all just stand here, not really knowing what to say.

"Why was he in Manson's office? Could they be a patient?" I ask no one in particular, I'm genuinely curious.

"I don't know," Manson says, running circles over Candy's hand. "We don't have cameras in the office, for privacy reasons, and the bookshop said he kept a hat on. Looking at the CCVT, he kept his head down."

"He left a note, with another puzzle piece," Creed states, jarring all of us by the looks on our faces, "I don't think he meant to leave them behind. They were in the door jam where Candy said she was stabbed."

"I didn't see that," I'm looking between the three of them. "How did you find it?"

"Nile found it," he corrects, lacing his fingers into mine and pulling me into his side.

"What did it say?" Manson and I both blurt, obviously sharing the same thought.

"And we have what? Three pieces now? Do you know what the photo is?"

"It said, 'this has only just begun', and whatever the image is, it's still unclear right now."

"This is the beginning?" I swallow, my chest heavy and my breaths shallow. How can this be the beginning? They killed two people, and almost killed Candy. How many more do they have planned?

Creed moves me from his side to his front and I bury my head in his chest.

"I have a whole team working on finding out what the image is," he smooths my hair down my shoulders. "My team also found a few fibers and hairs at the scene. They've been sent off for testing, if whoever is doing this is in any database we'll have a match."

I look up and him, brows skewed, "How do you have access to that?"

He looks at me as if I should know this, but I *just* learned about his mafia background. He needs to give me a break.

"Oh," I look away from him, laying my cheek on his chest, "Right."

"What are we going to do once we find out who's been behind all this?" Manson stands, stretching his limbs and filling a cup full of water to hand to Candy.

She smiles at him and he leans down to peck her lips.

"*We* aren't going to do anything," Creed warns and we all once again look at him, "This person is dangerous, borderline insane. There's nothing any of *you* can do."

"You don't mean that *you* will..." Manson trails off.

Creed doesn't say anything, instead he asks Manson if he needs to go home and change or shower. That we will stay with Candy while he takes care of himself. Of course Manson refuses, instead walking to where Creed and I stand.

He jerks his head toward the door, and Creed releases me, bending down and brushing a kiss against my temple, "We'll be right outside."

I nod, guessing Manson wants to speak to Creed alone.

Spinning around, I face Candy and really take a closer look at her. Her bruised face is yellow and green in places, and there are a few scrapes that are scabbed over on her forehead.

"How long was I actually out?" Candy asks waggling her eyebrows, "You two look comfy cozy."

My cheeks heat, but I'm not embarrassed. I'm happy, even though my best friend is right beside me laying in a hospital bed. My best friend was just stabbed three times, and I'm thinking about my sexy fun with Creed.

I'm the worst friend.

"Finally," she moves her head so she can see me through the hair that has shifted in front of my face.

We both let out a small laugh and I lean one hip against her bed. "He tongue fucked the shit out of me last night," I whisper. Candy smirks and coughs holding her side, and I immediately feel bad.

"You dirty girl!" She hollers while still laughing and not at all caring about the pain, "How was it?"

"It was," I let out a breath, motoring my lips, "Everything."

"You deserve to be happy, Ferny baby," she lays her hand on my hand, criss crossing her fingers with mine, "I mean it, this wasn't your fault, and I'm still here."

"You wouldn't be in the fucking hospital at all if I hadn't come back."

"No ma'am, no ham," she chuckles, "You are not allowed to withdraw because you have this sick sense of responsibility. You didn't make this psycho attack me, and kill people."

I look at our hands as she squeezes, as if she can crush it into my skin.

"You aren't the bad guy in this story," she tells me.

My eyes flick up to hers, they're hard, flinty, and I have this overwhelming sense of love for her. She has been through a vicious attack, yet here she is, making me feel better.

"When will you get to go home?"

"Manson says by the end of the week," she rolls her eyes, "I haven't been able to sleep well, so he's ready to build a hospital in the house so I can."

We both snicker, that sounds like something he would do. We continue to chat as the boys talk. She asks if I would check in on Fern and Flourished, and I promise I will. Creed probably won't let me go alone, so I'll drag him with me.

Finally they come back, Creed slaps Manson on the back and I kiss Candy's cheek, telling her I love her, and that I will call her when I've checked in on the bakery.

Creed guides me out with his hand on my back. I have my head down, looking at my feet when someone brushes my arm. Creed grumbles and pulls me closer to his side.

I look back, finding Dean looking at us.

"Dean?" I stop walking. "What are you doing here?"

This hospital is almost an hour away from Gravity Hill.

"I heard about Candy," he lifts his shoulders and opens one hand, "Thought I'd bring her a little something."

He has a small package wrapped in a silver paper topped with a bow in his hand.

"Why?" I ask, they haven't been friends since the night of my attack.

He laughs, looking between Creed and I, "Gretchen and I are engaged," he says, as if that somehow makes his appearance here any less weird, "She thought it would be nice to check on her boss."

Wow, him and Gretchen? That's a new development and an odd one, but who am I to judge love.

I step forward, holding out my palm. "She can't have visitors, only family, you understand," I squint my eyes against the sunlight glinting off the hospital doors. "I could give it to her."

No way am I letting him go in there, even if it is just to give her a gift.

He looks at the box and then back at me, Creed is still standing at my back, no doubt assessing the situation.

"Sure," he shrugs, placing the little box in my hand and winking before walking past us to his car.

I wrap my fingers around the box, and look at Creed, "That was weird, right?"

"Hasn't he always been a little different?"

I nod, because he had, maybe my mind is over analyzing everything now. I'm becoming suspicious of everyone who isn't my family.

Chapter Twenty-Five

Creed drives us to Fern and Flourished, where I unlock the back door with Manson's spare key he gave Creed, knowing Candy would ask one of us to check on the bakery. Turns out no dragging is required.

I can't remember the employee's names, other than Gretchen who is furiously working the register by herself. I watch the cameras in Candy's office for a minute, not sure how to help her.

The other three employees are buzzing around the kitchen, not paying us any attention as we walk through to the swinging door that separates the kitchen from the customer area.

Gretchen stops mid sentence when she spots us, asking the customer if she will excuse her for a moment. I can't help my eyes from looking at her ring finger on her left hand.

It's still fresh on my mind, sure enough there it is. An oval diamond, surprisingly modest for Dean's pockets. The way Gretchen latched onto Manson before, I'm shocked she settled for anything less than two carats.

"What are you doing here?" She is smiling, but her body language tells me everything I need to know. She is not happy to see me.

"Candy asked if we would check on the place," I tell her.

"Why?" She crosses her arms over her chest and taps her foot, "You don't know anything about it."

"I know that you're overwhelmed, where is your help?" I can ignore her bitchy attitude, I had for years before.

"Both of them called in this morning," she informs me, "But I have everything under control."

I look around, tables are dirty, with empty mugs and plates with crumbs. A line of customers waited, looping around to the door.

"Let me help you," I ask, because I know if I demand she will be stupid and tell me to fuck off.

I don't want to be here with her, but I also know Candy would do the same thing. She would jump head first into the fray and help.

Gretchen rolls her eyes, but relents. I look at Creed and he smirks, throwing a rag over his shoulder.

I walk to the part of the counter that lifts up so we can get out. We get started, me clearing the dishes while Creed wipes the tables down. He moves furniture back into place, wipes the leather down, all without complaint.

Once everything is clean, I offer to help Gretchen behind the counter, the point of sale system can't be too hard to figure out. She agrees, but I can tell it ate at her. Creed excuses himself when his phone rings, swiftly kissing my temple before walking to the back.

I assume to watch the cameras and take his phone call.

Turns out greeting customers and taking orders is much harder than I anticipated. I have no clue what any of the coffee orders are. What the hell is a flat white? If there wasn't a button on the machine that had the exact name, I was lost.

Thankfully the customers take pity on me and don't get too fancy with their orders. When the rush finally dies down, I wipe the counters clean.

"Thank you," Gretchen mutters, surprising me.

"You're welcome."

We stand there for a second in awkward silence, until I decide to walk around her and duck into the back. Before I get through fully she asks, "You haven't seen my brother, have you?"

I poke out my bottom lip. The last time I saw him was at brunch, but I think she means today. So I respond with, "No, why?"

She shakes her head, "It's nothing."

I nod, and continue to the back. One of the girls is speaking to the boy who smiled at me the last time I was here. When she sees me, she stops and picks up the icing bag she was using.

The boy sighs and rolls his eyes, "How is Candy?"

"She's okay," my eyes slide to him and back to her.

"Ignore Harley," he says, "She's worried about Candy, and she doesn't trust you."

I laugh, Harley's head snaps to where he is smirking and her mouth drops open.

"It's okay," I tell her, "I'm Fern."

"Oh, we know who you are," he crosses his arms over his chest. "The infamous Fern Hayes."

"I don't know about infamous."

Creed steps out of the office with a hard look on his face and nods to the door. I guess it's time to go.

Bidding them goodbye, we leave, locking the door behind ourselves.

Creed opens my door for me, making sure I am in and buckled before walking around and getting in himself.

Sitting there I feel how worked my muscles are, the delicious feeling of moving and doing something helpful. I love that feeling, maybe I will ask Candy for a job. I laugh at myself, and Creed looks at me questioningly.

"I was thinking I might ask Candy for a job."

"Why?"

"I liked today," I shrug.

"Well, then I guess you don't need the surprise waiting at home for you."

I jump in my seat, leaning forward to see his face, "Surprise?"

He laughs and nods, gripping my thigh, "Sit back."

I huff, but do as he asks. He runs his fingers up and down my leg, getting closer and closer to my pussy with every swipe. Leaning back against the headrest I watch him, his face giving nothing away, as if he doesn't know every time his fingers brush closer, that my breath hitches.

"What do you want, Charmer?" He rumbles.

"I want you to fuck me," I'm not about to be ashamed of the way I want him. There is no point, he knows already.

He groans, "Charmer."

"You asked."

"I should have known better," he teases, squeezing my thigh near my knee, electing a squeal. I'm extremely ticklish there.

Creed pulls the car up to the same gate Candy had when she brought me to her house. I eye him, confused, "We share a driveway."

He turns left, down another path. I was asleep the last time we made this drive, and this morning I was too keyed up to pay attention.

Seeing the house in the light of day was... magical. The colossal thing is made with brick and stone, arches hang over the double doors. The circle drive is pebbled in white stones.

"Holy shit," I whisper into the window, "I don't think I'll ever get used to this."

Luca comes out the front door, dressed in jeans and a t-shirt. It's an odd sight, I think I've only ever seen the man in a suit.

Creed parks the SUV in front of the doors and Luca jogs down the steps to open my door.

"You don't have to do that," I tell him, blushing at the thought of one of these men opening my door every time I come home.

He winks and nods at Creed.

The house is quiet, no boys linger in the living room as we walk through it to the back patio. The deck is large, just like the house. Twinkle lights strung from poles to the house, and I remember what they look like lit up.

I can't wait to sit out here one night and read, maybe

watch Creed swim a few laps in the pool.

We walk off the deck and onto the concrete patio that houses a basketball hoop, more furniture, and a covered kitchen. Walking into the grass we continue, his hand tangled with mine.

I don't know where to look, the rolling grass hills, or Manson and Candy's house off to the right. It looks bigger than before, but that is probably because of the different angle. We crest the top of a particularly tall hill and he stops, pulling me into his chest so my front is to a barn.

Not just any barn, of course, because Creed doesn't ever do anything half-assed. It's almost an exact replica of the barn at Rolling Oaks farm. The paint is new, and it doesn't have any chipped boards, but it's the same.

Familiar.

Black quilt patterns dot the outside of the structure, and the doors slide open. Noah steps out leading a horse that I would know anywhere. Daisy stands tall and proud as I turn around, with a big goofy grin on my face.

"You didn't."

"I did," he declares, releasing me so I can run to her. I hear his laugh all the way to the barn.

Daisy's chestnut coat is shiny and her posture is prominent. That's when I hear the clack of soft hoofs. She twists her neck, and I walk around, spotting the white and brown foal by her back leg.

"Daisy!" I speak, almost breathless, "He's beautiful!"

She nudges the middle of my shoulder blades, as if to tell me that it's okay to approach him. I hold out my hand, waiting for him to touch me first. He slowly shoves his nose into my fingers and I let out a laugh.

Running my hand up the soft fur of his nose to his ears, he moves closer to me, caging me in between him and his mother.

"You've got a good mama," I tell him, stroking the coarse hair on his neck. Daisy hits my back with her snout, and I turn so I can rub them both.

Creed and I lock eyes, and I can't help the tears that begin to pool. This is a dream, a dream life.

"You did all of this, for me?"

He nods, and walks closer. Daisy swings her head around, leveling him with a stare.

"He's a good one," I whisper to her, turning to introduce them. Standing in front of Creed, between him and Daisy I hold his hand, guiding it to her nose and letting her judge him.

She does, and he runs his hand down her neck and pats her chest, "She'll fit in just fine around here."

My smile is infectious as we lead her further out to the ring beside the barn. The ground has been covered in fresh sandy dirt, and once the gate is closed she trots. Watching horses isn't something I ever thought I'd miss.

But the way their muscles move in their powerful bodies is astounding. I can't wait to saddle her and ride. Feeling the wind whipping my hair, and the freeness of it.

Noah hops up on the fence, "Everything that used to be yours at the ranch is here now."

"Thank you."

"He'll take good care of you," he tips his head toward where Creed is leaning against the bars. "But, if you need me, you know how to reach me."

"I know," I tell him.

"I'm leavin' again soon, gotta get on the road," he faces me, wrapping an arm around my shoulders he quickly squeezes and lets go. "Take care of yourself Fern, and name that foal."

He hops down, shaking Creed's hand and walking back up to the house.

Creed walks to where I still sit on the bars, leaning his elbows around my hips and enjoying the view. We don't speak, words aren't really needed, he knows what this means to me. I spent two years of my life on the ranch, working and healing.

Daisy is my reminder that I can survive anything.

When the sun starts to set Creed helps me lead Daisy in, I haven't thought of a name for Daisy's baby yet. That will come to me in time, for now I'm happy to load them into their stall and let them rest.

With a few last pets and some apple slices, I promise to return and close up the barn with Creed. I kiss him after the doors are latched, throwing my arms around him and climbing his body.

He places his arms under my legs and situates me against his body, backing us up so my back hits the wooden siding. I hook my ankles together, holding him against me as his tongue strokes mine.

We take our time, hands searching each other's bodies as our lips connect.

"We should take this inside," he breaths against my mouth. "Before I fuck you for the first time against a barn."

"Take me inside," I agree.

We walk hand in hand to the house where he pushes me up against the glass, under the glowing twinkle lights.

His hand runs from my torso to my neck where he flexes his fingers around my pulse, teasing his lips across mine. The house is silent still as he slides the door open behind me. Walking me backward to the stairs as he plants kisses along my neck.

I giggle and run up the stairs, feeling like a teenager again. His footsteps pound after mine. Sticking my finger on the scanner for the door, I wait, listening to him slowly make his way down the hall.

The door pops open and I push it further, running in and kicking my shoes off. He catches my arm as I start toward the bedroom.

"That's my job, baby."

I smirk, "Dragging it out, huh?"

"I've waited for this moment for a long time," his chest rumbles against mine, "And I plan to savor every fucking second."

His fists bunches up the material of my dress, exposing my legs as he drags the cloth up my body. He runs his other hand over my thigh, squeezing the plump flesh, growling low in his throat, "I love your body, Fern."

I let my head fall back as he continues his caress. His hands move higher, tracing the faint lines of my skin that I've always loved. Pushing the dress up and over my breasts he shuts his eyes, inhaling my skin.

He drops kisses over the swells of my breasts, trailing them up to my shoulder, and catching on to my ear lobe. Turning my head to catch his mouth with mine, I thread my fingers through his wavy hair, pulling him closer.

Running my hands down his neck and over his shoulders I grip him, "show me how much."

I rush to pull the dress over my head, I'm proud of all the dips and dents in my skin, and with him staring at me like I'm the last drink of water in a dessert, it makes me bolder.

His hands slip the straps of my bra down my shoulders to rest on my arms, before he uses one hand to unhook the clasps. My breasts spill free between us, and his hands immediately go to them, "I didn't get to properly appreciate these last night."

He plays with my nipples, turning them into harder pebbles. Bending down and capturing one in his mouth, sucking and biting. The slight sting of it makes me blush and moan.

Releasing my nipple he croaks, "I fucking love those sounds," before going to the other and showing it the same amount of attention. I am so wet, I have to rub my legs together just to get some release.

While he's enjoying my breasts, his hands run over the expanse of my stomach, down to my thong. The strap is rolled up on one side, but I don't have time to be embarrassed. He releases my breasts and hooks his fingers into the band. Shimming them down my legs where he kneels, and goddamn if he doesn't look fucking magnificent.

This man, on his knees for *me*.

With his eyes on mine he licks a path up the length of my pussy. He is hypnotizing, using his tongue to carve out his name. His hand grips my leg, and he places it over one shoulder so I have to support myself on one leg.

I'm going to fall, but fuck me, I don't want him to stop.

The second the thought crosses my mind he unhooks my leg from his shoulder and stands, slamming his lips to mine. My taste is on his tongue driving me wild. I can't think, don't want to as he picks me up by my ass and carries me to the bed.

"I think you have an unfair advantage," I drawl. "Here I am, naked in our bed, and yet there you stand, clothed."

He laughs, "I guess I'd better remedy that."

I nod vigorously, I've only seen him naked once, so I haven't gotten the chance to appreciate his body. Slowly he unbuttons his shirt, tossing it to the side and reaching behind his neck to pull his undershirt off with one hand. I'm one breathless bitch. He is packed with muscles that I know he worked for, but hot damn, I don't think I'll ever get used to it.

His buckle clicks as he undoes the leather and pulls it out of his slacks. He watches me as he drops his pants and steps out of them. In just his boxers and socks he is a sight. Dark hair covers his legs and paints a sinful trail down his torso to the bulge in his underwear.

I bite my lip, letting it go slowly, holding my breath. I want to see him, touch him, taste him.

I want all the things.

"You look hungry, baby," his voice is like cool silk brushing over my bare skin. I moaned, and when his boxers come off I'm pretty fucking sure I start drooling. Thick, standing tall and proud, his cock is mouthwatering.

"So fucking hungry," I slide to the edge of the bed, gently lowering myself to the floor. "May I?"

"Fuck yes," his breath stutters. "You can touch me anytime, anywhere, Charmer."

Leaning in, I lick him from root to tip. He shudders and places a hand on my hair. Circling his tip with my tongue as his fingers dive into my strands. With my hands I grip the base of his cock and slowly stroke him to his tip. He groans as I open my mouth, sticking out my tongue and guiding him there.

I lick the bead of pre-cum off the crown of his cock, humming in excitement, before closing my lips around him. I flick the underside of his cock, teasing and working him further into my mouth. His whole body vibrates while I bob my head, taking him deeper as his grip tightens on my hair.

He pulls my head back, yanking the hair at the base of my skull, "As much as I'm enjoying this, baby, I need to be inside of you or this will be over before it really starts."

Picking me up, he places me on the bed, positioning himself over me. His cock wet as he slides it through my pussy. I moan as he rubs my clit with the end of his dick.

Slowly he eases himself inside of me, green eyes locked with mine. I wince at the fullness of him, and he bends down to kiss me.

"We'll go slow," he promises. "You can take it."

He works himself in and out, going deeper with every tender thrust until he is fully seated inside of me. I pull in a deep breath as he starts to move. Softly grinding, getting me used to his size.

I'm so fucking wet, it's easy for him to glide in and out, testing my limits.

"Lift your hips," he murmurs, grabbing a pillow from the head of the bed. He wedges it under my ass and eases back in. Hitting a whole new angle that has me closing my eyes and whimpering.

"Eyes on me, baby."

I pop them back open, and watch him maneuvering his hips while he brings me to the precipice of release.

"Creed," I sigh, I'm lost in him. The way he brushes against my clit with every thrust, hitting a spot inside of my body that lights up all my nerves.

He bends down to kiss me, never breaking his rhythm. His hips snap into mine over and over as we devour each other. My hands on his back, squeezing and clawing at his skin. With one of his hands on my hip and the other in my hair, he whispers against my lips, "Let go, Charmer."

A lone tear escapes as I shatter underneath him. I writhe and moan as release barrels through me like none other. My muscles lock up, and I kiss him, panting into his mouth.

Heat flushes through my body as he drives me higher, plunging his cock in and out of my pussy.

"My turn, baby." He lifts one of my legs, placing it on his shoulder as he rides out his pleasure, coming hard.

"*Fuuuuck*." He grunts, pulling out and fisting himself until ropes of cum pour from him and paint my chest.

His whole body trembles as he stills and groans, rolling to his side and going to the bathroom, he brings back a damp washcloth to clean me up. When he is satisfied he brings me to him by my leg. We don't need to speak, our bodies said everything we already know to be true.

I cuddle into his side, basking in the glow of an orgasm and finally having him. The man I have always wanted, but couldn't have.

Or so I thought.

As my eyes drift closed, a memory surfaces.

It makes me laugh as I snuggle in closer, I was bold, couldn't argue that.

"Do you remember that Halloween when you found me at a party and brought me home?"

"How could I forget? The inmate costume had me hard the whole ride back to your house."

I giggle thinking back, little Fern would have gotten a kick out of that.

"In the car, when you said I looked good...were you flirting with me?"

He groans, "Yes, Charmer, but since you had to ask that just now, I guess you really didn't notice any of the *other* times I attempted it."

I laugh, throwing my head back and shaking.

"If I would have known," I admit.

"We would still end up here," he declares with such confidence, and it makes me tingly.

"The memory of that kiss is what kept me going while I was with my father."

I smile and burrow into his chest.

I'm almost asleep when I think I heard the doorbell ring,

but Creed doesn't move from where he has me swaddled in the blankets and his body. So I ignore it, and drift into oblivion.

Chapter Twenty-Six

Candy and I had gone out on Halloween of our junior year. We were dressed as slutty inmates. It wasn't unusual for us to flaunt a little skin, and Candy had been invited to a neighboring college party. I was nervous that we might run into my brother, who would ruin all of our fun, by demanding that we go home.

Gravity U wasn't that far from home, and Candy really wanted to go. She met a GU boy at the market downtown and hit it off with him. So, being the friend I am, we went. The house we arrived at was full to the brim with people drinking, smoking, or snorting whatever they could get their hands on.

The guy Candy met found us quickly and draped his arm around our shoulders.

"Don't worry, ladies," he smelt of cheap beer and weed, "I'll show you around."

I wasn't particularly worried about being shown around.

I could find anything I needed, without a guide. I shrugged his arm off, and followed them inside. They quickly found the dance floor and melted into the crowd.

No matter, I carved my way through the house, looking for the kitchen. I needed a drink. There was a crowd cheering on a game of beer pong in the way of the coolers. I didn't drink alcohol, it was a choice I had made freshman year when I saw Manson swaying on his feet sneaking into his bedroom.

I couldn't lose control.

"Hey inmate!" Someone hollered as I slowly cut my way through the onlookers.

Continuing on my way, I finally got to the coolers, lifting the lid only to find more beer, and wine coolers. The cooler was blocking the fridge, so I shoved it aside and opened the door. Cool air hit my skin, and I found what I was looking for.

Water bottles lined the top shelf, I stood on my tippy toes and swiped a bottle. Cracking the seal I took a few healthy swallows, and heard the unmistakable voice of Creed.

Fuck. This was bad. If he was here, Manson was here, and if Manson was here Candy and I needed to get out. I really didn't want to put on a show for anyone's viewing pleasure tonight.

I scanned the crowd, looking for him. I couldn't help it,

he was like a magnet for me. The north to my south, and he didn't even fucking notice me.

He was standing behind the make-shift beer pong table they constructed out of the kitchen island. Again, the loud asshole shouted, "Hey inmate, come show me a good time."

I rolled my eyes and started toward the back door when my body went hot and my stomach dropped.

"You shouldn't be here," Creed said, hot on my heels.

He followed me to the back yard where minimal people were milling about and smoke clung to the air.

"Last time I checked, I didn't need your permission to do anything," I quipped, placing my hands on my hips.

"Where are your clothes, Charmer?" He asked, eyes scanning my body.

"I'm wearing them," I did a spin so he could see that all of my bits were covered, more than a bathing suit did anyway.

He slid his jacket off his shoulders and handed it to me. When I didn't immediately reach out to take it, he stepped into my space, "Put it on, or I'll put it on for you."

I crossed my arms, he wasn't about to tell me what to do.

"I think I'll pass, thank you."

Striding to the back door I was halted by my hair. He did not. I spun, ready to kick him in the shins if I had to.

"What the fuck, Creed?"

With me dumbfounded, he took the opportunity to slip the jacket over my arms, closing it and zipping it.

"I warned you."

His face was millimeters from mine, and my breaths stalled. His eyes dipped down to my lips, and mine did the same to his.

Thunder cracked and the sky opened up, rain poured down, soaking everyone who was now trying to get inside. He gripped my upper arm, pulling me into his arms and walking us toward a side entrance where cars were parked.

He opened one of the doors and shoved me in, walking around the hood and sitting in the driver's seat.

"Candy," I protested.

"Manson already found her, how do you think I knew to look for you?"

Damn it.

He shoved the car in reverse and peeled out of the drive. After a few blocks he said, "You look good tonight, Charmer."

I rolled my eyes, he was just being nice because he ruined my night. When we got back to the house he opened an umbrella and held it over me as we walked up the steps to the door.

"I can hold my own fucking umbrella," I grumbled.

"Well aware," he bent down into my bubble, "But maybe you could let me be a gentleman for once."

He was so close to my lips, and fuck it, I swallowed down my fear and planted my lips on his. I wasn't going to lose another chance.

At first he didn't react, standing stock still. Until he dropped the umbrella, pulled me into his arms and pressed his body against mine, pinning me against the door. Kissing me back with everything I was giving him. His kiss sent shock waves through my system, and I gasped into his mouth.

That seemed to break him out of his fog and he settled his forehead against mine before stepping back. He rubbed a hand down the back of his neck, but remained silent.

I was waiting for him to tell me that it was a mistake, of all the reasons he shouldn't have kissed me.

Instead he turned around and walked away.

Chapter Twenty-Seven

I'm deliciously sore, toasty, and more satisfied than I ever have been before. Last night was tender and would forever be ingrained in my memory. Throwing my hands up over my head to stretch I kick out, shaking my muscles.

Creed isn't here, but I figure with keeping me company all day yesterday he has business he needs to attend to.

I take my time getting out of bed, enjoying the soft carpet beneath my feet and taking it all in. Going to the bathroom I decide on a quick shower, the water perfectly scalding as I wash and get out.

My clothes have been put away, I didn't notice last night when Creed and I got back. Prancing around naked feels like a moment of acceptance, like the last piece that I needed for things to fall into place.

I'm home.

Tittering, I go to the closet and pull on my favorite pair of yoga pants and t-shirt. I don't want to leave the property today. A day in feels necessary.

Traveling down the stairs I listen to the boys, but I notice one of them is missing. Their bickering is funny and reminds me of younger versions of Manson and I.

"Don't y'all go to school?" I ask and all of their heads swivel in my direction when I pause on the bottom step. "And where are your mothers?"

Someone clears their throat and I turn to find a man I don't recognize standing near the front door.

"They do have school," he says, his voice harsh, "but it's their break." They scatter right as the missing one turns up with a plate full of nachos and drinks hanging from his mouth. His eyes go wide when he spots us and he retreats back to the kitchen.

"We haven't officially met," he stands there not making any move to step closer. "My name is Diego."

I remember the name, one of the men Creed trusted with his life.

"Nice to meet you," I step down from the stairs and offer my hand. He doesn't take it, but then I notice the burn scars on his hands. They cover his fingers, all the way up to where nails should be. I try not to stare, really I do, but it looks awful, the pain he must have gone through...

"Creed asked if I'd come get you, something has come

up."

"Candy?" I panic and shout.

He doesn't answer, just stalks his way toward the hallway beneath the stairs.

"Give me a second, I need some water," I say, deviating from his path to head into the kitchen. I need something to drink before I face whatever is waiting, and the filter system in this house is unmatched. The fridge is near a crook in the wall where the coffee bar is inlaid, and there is a small window at the coffee bar that looks into the pantry.

Grabbing a glass from the cabinet closest to the fridge, I press the button on the front to fill the glass and pause, eyes popping from my face. Henry and Banks are in the pantry, locked in a tight embrace, nachos and snacks forgotten on the bar beside them.

Kissing.

Devouring each other, as if it's the last time they will touch. My eyes are wide, and I feel like the biggest creep alive. Leaving the glass and hurrying out, so they don't catch me during their... moment.

I thump off of Diego's body after exiting the kitchen, his eyes glimpse to my empty hands and I wave them around awkwardly because... shit, what the hell was I going to say?

"Changed my mind," I couldn't shut my mind off after the

intrusion. I don't speak, unsure of what else to say. What happens now?

I don't have to wait long, I can hear Creed talking to someone else in the room, "How did this happen?"

I let Diego lead me to the security room where I immediately notice a wall covered in monitors. My husband is standing in front of them, with Luca and Nile on either side of him.

Creed turns around, and I can tell by the way he looks at me, that whatever is on those monitors is not good. He nods to Luca to shut the monitors off before I can see anything else.

"Good morning, Charmer."

"What happened?" I ask.

He sighs and swipes a hand down his face, "Guys, could you clear the room."

They all leave, the second the words leave his mouth, "I want that superpower."

"Baby, do you know Garrett Walker?"

"Yeah," he's Gretchen's twin, she asked about him yesterday, "I saw him at the restaurant the other day at brunch with Dean, and I kissed him a few years ago...why?"

He leans back in his chair and beckons me over with two fingers. Crossing the room and rounding the desk I go to him. He pulls me into his lap and kisses my neck.

"He turned up on our front steps."

I lift his head with my hand on his jaw, "Where is he now?"

"He wasn't alive when we got to him," he waits for me to say something, but I don't know what to say, my heart is breaking. My eyes slip closed as tears threaten to spill over.

"That's not the worst part."

"There's something worse than a dead body on our door step?"

"His lips were surgically removed."

My eyes pop open, because what the fuck.

"And then his mouth was sewn together so he couldn't speak."

"Like that zombie with those three witches sewn?" I ask, I'm quickly starting to freak out. Who would surgically remove someone's lips?

He nods and adds, "He had them in a box."

"His lips?" I choke out, feeling my stomach wanting to give. I'm glad I haven't eaten.

"We moved him, but for the time being I don't want you leaving the house," he folds his arms around my hips.

I watch the camera feeds flip between different parts of the property, "I want to see it."

He sighs deeply, "That's not a good idea, Charmer."

"I appreciate that you want to protect me, but I need to see it."

"I don't like this," he mutters, double clicking on an image at the bottom right on his screen, and bringing up a black and white video, muted.

"I want to hear it."

"Baby," he sounds like he wants to plead, "Those sounds will haunt your days and nights."

"What if we hear something in the video that gives us a clue?"

"We all listened, and we didn't hear anything other than a man dying."

I was locked on the screen, I needed this, and I think he could tell. It didn't mean that I would be okay, but I was tired of people dying around me.

He hit the volume and turned it up, then hit play. Placing me between his legs, he kept his arms around me, as if to hold me together.

It was dark so the video has a slight green quality to it.

Garrett shows up on the screen, far enough away that I'm not sure if it's him or just a blip on the screen. It moves closer, slowly and gravel crunches under his boots. His clothes are dark against the white pebbles.

He staggers, zigzagging as he limps his way to the door,

grunting and moaning in pain with every move. When he gets closer, I can see the crude way someone stitched his mouth together.

Angry red tissue puffs and forms around the horrific stitching that's still bleeding and running down his chin and neck. He gurgles, as if choking on something, and my heart hits my stomach. His clothes look torn and as he approaches the door, I can see the box in his hand that I assume holds his lips.

His movements are slowing down, as he leaves a trail of blood behind his footsteps. Droplets hit the ground as my heart hammers in time with them.

Jesus, he's bleeding so much I can't understand how he's still up right. He has to be woozy, light headed and disoriented.

Muffled screams start after the doorbell goes off, his arm falls as he hits his knees, collapsing face first on the stone. I look toward Creed, confused about what just happened.

"His heart gave out."

"Oh my God," I gasp through my fingers, "Who could do something like this?"

Creed clicks off the screen and turns me around, placing me on the desk so I don't have to stand. He rises, standing between my legs, "That's not all…"

"A man had his lips removed and put in a fucking box, Creed! What more could there be?"

He takes a deep breath, handing me a slip of wet paper covered in blood and..*oh God*

> IT DISGUSTED ME THEN
> WATCHING YOUR LIPS TOUCH HIS
> YOU SHOULD NEVER HAVE DONE IT
> NOW HE'LL FOREVER BE MISSED

"Nile cut Garretts mouth open, and bingo," he pauses to push my hair back behind my ear, "We've got almost all of the pieces now, do you think you could look at it?"

I nod, still processing the terror Garrett had to be feeling before he bled out on my doorstep. He was alone, and in so much pain. I let myself wheeze for a second, he must have been scared and miserable.

"Hey, baby," his hands are warm on my cheeks. "We are going to figure this out."

I shake my head, because that's all I can do. He walks me to a room with red tape on the walls, tables covered in newspapers, police reports, and photos of bodies. Where the rest of the posse is currently pouring over clues.

"Is this..." I trail off.

"It's everything we have on whoever this is."

The wall has characteristics labeled over an anonymous picture. The puzzle pieces are put together on a table clear of anything but the puzzle itself. The image is blurry, but I can clearly tell the half naked woman in it is me.

Creed's hands open and close by his sides, I guess he knows it too. But the person beside me, the face is missing. Whoever it is could be the next victim, or the killer.

"Who's with you?" Creed thunders softly.

"I can't remember."

Whoever it is, they are clearly younger. I can't have been more than seventeen, and I hadn't been with that many people back then. Why can I not remember? They're male, dressed in nice jeans and a polo. Their watch looks expensive, but the blankets are blank and white.

"We're in a truck," I say, pointing to the wheel covering. It's navy, a color that isn't too popular around here.

Creed and the other men start discussing the new information as I stare at the image. It will bother me, not being able to figure it out.

I focus everything I have into that image and the words tacked to the wall. Tall, sporty, influence. I'm not certain about the influence part, since Creed and his friends have been cleaning up their messes.

Looking back to the picture, I think back to high school. I used to go out to the mountain passes all the time with Candy. I hooked up with a lot of people, some guys, some girls. I wasn't picky.

Nothing stands out, other than Garrett and me kissing the same night Gray and I were attacked. Garrett had kissed me before, but that night we put on a show. Candy and I have made out more times than I can count. What if this person isn't after me to hurt me, but to hurt the people I have been sexual with?

Creed's head pops up and I shrink a little, "Did I say that out loud?"

He nods but tilts his head, "Did you fuck Garrett?"

"No, never," I'm sure of that, "Gray is the only one this person has gone after that I'd ever had sex with."

"For now," chirps one of the boys standing in the doorway.

"Not helpful, Talon," Nile grumbles. "What are you doing in here?"

"I came to tell you someone is at the gate, asking for Creed."

Creed stands, shooting his eyes in my direction as if telling me to stay, and walks out behind Talon.

It takes him a while before I hear his steps coming back through the house.

"Everything okay, boss?"

"Charmer," he nods to Nile who'd asked the question, "Can you go upstairs and get dressed?"

I don't ask why, even though I really want to. His features are stern and I get the feeling that he won't answer me anyway. Not until we aren't in the same room with his men.

Is it another body?

Candy?

My mind splinters with thoughts and questions.

Sweeping past him I walk upstairs, the boys are sitting on the couch talking amongst themselves. I guess whoever it was they know them because they don't seem ruffled. Their video game is paused and I think once again about their mothers.

I don't ask this time though, instead I go to our room and change into a white pants suit that flares at my feet and drops low enough to show off my ample cleavage. I pair that with a pair of heels that match my bralette.

I'll slay all
your
demons I ignite
all your
dreams
I only want
what's best
For us to be
free
We'll be the
king and queen
If you'll stay
with me

Chapter Twenty-Eight

Creed comes up not long after, changing into a gray button down he stops when I stand.

"Change," he demands.

"Excuse me?" I cock my head to the side, unsure how he thinks he has any say in my clothes.

"We're going to a meeting," he rubs his forefinger and thumb over his brow. "My father and brother are here."

"Again," I suck in a breath, "Excuse me?"

"They want to meet you, and since I called a meeting after Garrett showed up, they flew down."

"How could they have gotten here so fast?" I'm astounded at the efficiency.

"Private jet," he scoffs, "Put on a dress."

"Why?"

"Charmer, please."

Annoyance settles in my brain, he is being such a prick.

Over my outfit.

I huff and walk back to the closet, unsure of which dress I want to pick. I have a few that are probably dressy enough. Pulling out a dark cherry short dress I smile to myself, why not. If I'm going to a mafia meeting, I might as well wear red.

Not only that, but it's short enough that if I bend over everyone will see my ass. Take *that* husband.

The dress slips up my legs smoothly as I wiggle it over my hips and zip it as far as I can without help. It is form fitting in the bodice, with a matching lace overlay. The skirt is tulle, flowing down to my knees.

The shoes I picked out before are black so I put them back on. Stepping out of the closet I find Creed rolling up his sleeves.

He crosses the room, slipping his arms around my waist and pulling us so our bodies are flush, "I'm one lucky asshole."

"You said it," I laughed, as he bent down to kiss me.

"After this we can do whatever you want."

"Okay," I step back and twirl so he can see the whole thing, "Zip me up?"

He does, nimble fingers closing the gap I couldn't.

"You're so beautiful," he pulls me through the room and to the car. Luca, Nile and Diego are already in another one, along with their sons.

We take off out of the garage, Luca hot on our heels in his bigger SUV. The gates roll open and closed as we go through and I wonder if there is a sensor in the car, or if it's motion controlled.

"There's something that's been bugging me," I ask looking out the window, thinking about the boys, "Where are the boys' mothers?"

He takes a deep breath, "Toby and Talon's mother took off after they were about three, Talon has always had a mean streak, and she just couldn't handle it. Henry's mother died giving birth to him, and Banks' was killed in a home invasion."

"Those poor boys," I thought their mothers just lived elsewhere, like Creed's mother had.

"They're good boys, most of the time."

"They have four fathers looking out for them," I chuckle.

His eyes slide to mine, "And now they have you."

It's huge shoes to fill, I don't even know if I want kids, and they are all nearly grown, almost out of high school. I can't imagine they will want me looking after them. My mind wanders at the new information, going back and forth from Garrett, Gray, and Candy. I watch the world pass by as we make our way to wherever we're going in silence.

The restaurant Creed brings us to has a back entrance

where he parks his SUV. I've been here a time or two with my family, but never with Creed, and never to a mafia meeting.

"I'm nervous," I admit, flattening out my dress.

He glances at me out of the corner of his eye, "Because my family wants to meet you?"

I inhale suddenly in disbelief, rolling my eyes. He is in the mafia, and not just in it, but a leader's son. His roots are tangled so deep I can't imagine he will ever get out. Even if he wants to.

I groan and then squeak when Creed pulls my chin to look at him, snapping me out of my nerves.

"If you make that sound again I'll force my entire family to wait while I fuck it out of you over and over," he growls.

Promises, promises, "In front of all of your friends?"

"I would fuck you anywhere you'd let me," he smirked.

"I've never met a mob boss," I say, changing the subject. If he keeps going like he is, we won't ever make it to the meeting... well we will, we'll just be very late.

He stills, flexing his fingers on the steering wheel, "Don't say that inside, okay?"

"Okay, so you want me to be the seen and not heard type of woman?" I know I shouldn't have said it the second it came out of my mouth.

His head swivels to face me so fast it's a wonder his neck didn't crack, "I would never expect you to keep your mouth shut, but these men aren't used to…sharp mouthed women, and you are as sharp as they come."

"So what do I do?"

"Be yourself, just don't call anyone by anything except the name they give you, and don't mention Bridgett."

His mention of that night jars me, but I'd forgotten he told me about her, and that night. How that was a bad night for not only him, but also his brother.

I can't stop seeing the video from the cameras. The way Garrett looked with his eyes left open and staring into the night sky. How the blood dripped down his chin and his lips had been flayed from his face.

Creed sighs, pulling me out from under those thoughts. He runs his hand down his face and says, "I'm sorry."

I bury my face in his shoulder, I just want this nightmare to be over.

Creed strokes his hand over my hair, "I promise, we're going to catch this bastard, and he'll never scare you again."

I peek an eye out to see the savage look on his face. I know he's serious, he isn't ever not serious when it comes to me.

Especially since Garrett's body showed up at our house with the rest of the puzzle pieces.

Well... almost all.

He releases the catch on the door and the lock pops up, but I don't dare touch it. He likes to open my doors. I watch him adjust his shirt sleeves and speak to his friends.

I have always been attracted to Creed, even when I was too young to know what to call it. The way his eyes burn when he looks at me, the subtle movements he makes when I move. Like our bodies have always been twined together by fate herself.

"Don't look at me like that, Charmer," he says, pulling open my door.

"It's how I always look at you," I tell him, because it is.

"No," he releases the door behind me, shutting and locking it, "It's not."

We don't speak as he guides me behind the others through the door and through what looks like a storage room. A man dressed impeccably holds the door to a kitchen open in front of us and Creed steps in front of me to greet him with a nod.

The man nods, but doesn't speak as he follows us to wherever Creed is leading. Another door off the kitchen opens to a small room with a few tables scattered throughout. It would be cozy if it weren't for the men sitting at the table.

They are large men, much like Creed. All dressed in button downs with varying tattoos peeking out from rolled up sleeves. Two of them look suspiciously like Creed, and I know immediately who they are.

They all nod as Creed places me into the only seat left at the table. A waiter brings in another chair as Creed pushes mine in, caging me in at the table.

I survey the men, noticing all the ink and muscles in the room. I don't speak, instead I wait, just like everyone else. Creed cracks his knuckles and begins, "A lot of you have been waiting to meet my wife," he looks at me then, "This is Fern Hemlock."

It's a shock to hear my first name mixed with his last name. Like I had forgotten that we are actually married.

The men lean forward, but I refuse to cower under their stares, "Nice to meet you all."

Only his brother continues to look at me as Creed takes over the conversation.

"I've asked for a meeting today because I need each of you on the streets," he stops when one of the men taps a finger on the table. Creed nods to him and the man speaks.

"Why should we care, what do these bodies have to do with us?"

"We don't pay you to ask stupid questions," Creed answers

smoothly. "As I was saying, twice now this bastard has killed and the police are fucking inept."

"We shouldn't speak of such ilk in front of the lady," the man beside the first speaks up, and I immediately like him. He's scary and has a small scar on his throat that bubbles and moves when he speaks, as if someone tried carving his Adam's apple out of his neck.

I grin in Creed's direction, because *yeah*, I shouldn't be here for this talk. I don't want to think about it, much less be reminded in a room full of men I would have gladly fucked for fun before this whole mess started.

Creed's eyes narrow, on me and one brow arches on his beautiful face. A challenge clearly.

"The lady is fine," he says, eyes still trained on me.

They dissolve into conversation as I scan the room, tuning out all the details he is going over. The other tables are smaller and unoccupied, one looked like a poker table in the corner of the room.

I feel it the second Creed's attention is back on me. The fire that licks through my body when his eyes are on my body. His hand slides over his thigh and onto mine. He is listening to whatever the other men are saying, but my ears are roaring with blood rushing through my head.

He squeezes my leg, kneading the tissue there and going

higher, up and up. I freeze, unbelieving that he is touching me, publicly. It may be under a table covered in cloth, but he is moving dangerously close to my pussy.

I gasp as his hand reaches under my dress and finds me bare. I hate underwear, always have. It gets in the way, and it's uncomfortable, but I didn't think he would be this bold with his family sitting here.

"Luca," he says, one word and all three of his men, plus the boys are up and out of their seats. They collect the two who I clocked as Creed's brother and father, leading them from the room, leaving only unfamiliar men at the table.

My hands cover Creed's roaming hand before he can do anything else to my already fragile mind. He threatened this, but God, I never imagined that he actually would.

Since I moved in, we have been pretty handsy, but never in my wildest dreams did I think he would do *this*. He grips my fingers tightly in his hand, placing them gently on the opposite side of my body.

Slowly he trails his hand back to where it was before. He strokes my cunt, lips tipping up in a knowing smirk. I'm wet, and I have been since his comment in the car.

He answers one of the guys as if he isn't busy driving me wild with anticipation and fear.

His fingers glide easily through my wetness and I chance

a glance around the room. None of the unfamiliar men are watching us, instead their faces look focus on their current topic.

I try not to squirm as he plunges one finger into my pussy, softly stroking my clit with the heel of his hand. The calloused digits pull back and he notches another at my entrance, a small warning before he fills me again.

He leans down, "you have ten seconds to come on my fingers," he growls as he continues pumping his fingers in and out of me under the table. "Or I'll throw you on top of this table and have these men watch as I fuck you until your screaming."

He starts to softly count as I try not to writhe and draw attention to what he is doing.

"Ten," I can't focus on his fingers as the sounds of my arousal fill the air. A flush climbs up my cheeks, knowing his men can hear his fingers in my pussy.

"Nine."

"Please," I whimper as quietly as I can. I won't be able to come like this. No matter how well his calloused fingers work my pussy.

He grins as he answers another question from one of the men. "Six, Charmer," he reminds me.

My senses are on overdrive, trying to avoid the looks

being thrown my way. My legs clench his wrist, trying to stop his movements and he growls.

"Try and stop me again, baby," his smile turns wolfish, his teeth gleaming, "Times up."

Excitement and uncertainty mingle in my stomach as he pulls me up and out of my seat. My dress falls, covering me before he deposits me on the table. My ass bounces against the hardwood, "Creed," I try to reason with him.

"Uh-uh, Charmer. You knew what I wanted, and you didn't give it to me," he chides, as if we aren't surrounded by a table full of gangsters speaking casually about the killer on the loose.

"Now, take your punishment like the little whore I know you are."

His hand splays over my chest as he pushes me down so my back is flat against the table. I turn my head to avoid his stare and catch the man with the scar licking his lips.

Oh God, what have I done?

Quickly, I turn my head back to where Creed is unbuckling his belt, he whips it out of the loops in one fluid motion. Sending a rush of heat through my body. Impossibly, more wetness gathers. I'm so fucking turned on, and I'm not embarrassed by it.

He throws the leather into the chair behind him and

frees his cock from his slacks pumping it with one of those tattooed hands that I love so much.

He doesn't give me any warning as he slams straight into my dripping pussy. His hips sitting flush with mine as I let out a cry. He leans over me, pressing one hand into the table by my head and the other around my throat.

"You love this, don't you, Charmer?" he whispers into my ear. His beard scratches my jaw and his voice rumbles my insides, "My cock buried between your thighs while these men all watch."

I nod against his hand, eagerly. Because I do love it, the depravity of it, the twisted parts of me I thought I lost are still here. Still beating under my skin, I just needed *him* to bring them back out. He adjusts my leg so it's wrapped around his back, eliciting a moan from low in my throat.

"There she is," Creed croons, "My dirty little plaything who likes to put on a show."

My brain short circuits as I hear grunts around me. The men watching can't see my sex, yet I know they're getting glimpses of my ass. The way Creed has me positioned they would have to be behind him to see the way my cunt is dripping with my impending orgasm. I'm spiraling as he continues to punish me with deep even thrusts.

"Show them how much you fucking love my cock, baby.

Scream for me."

I scream as my release barrels through me, throwing my head back as far as I can while Creed puts just enough pressure on my throat to have me gasping for air.

"Good girl," he praises as he lifts up and continues thrusting into my body. Our skin slapping together as he works me harder and harder. His hand leaves my throat and he wraps them both around my full hips as he lifts me. Hitting another spot deep inside that has my body coiling tighter. "One more time baby, and I expect you to fucking ruin my pants. Got me?"

I can't speak, not with the fire burning low inside of my belly. I lift my arms above my head and gripped the edge of the table. No longer caring that his men are here and enjoying every filthy fucking thing he is saying and doing.

Creed drags one arm under my ass to support his position while the other hand is free to rub hard and fast circles over my clit.

Goddamn, he is going to kill me. I moan, low and loud.

"That's it," he rumbles, while my inner walls clench and squeeze him. "I want them to see just how hard you fucking come on my cock, and *only* my cock."

"Creed!" I shout his name as my orgasm explodes through my whole body. Everywhere and I can't breathe as my cunt spasms and squirts all over his cock and hips. The rush of cum spraying all over him and the floor as he continues to fuck me should be embarrassing, but it feels too fucking good for me to care. I moan and squeeze the table as if I'll break it.

My body quivers as his dick twitches and he continues his assault on my clit, wringing every last drop of my orgasm from me. He spills inside of me with a sexy as fuck groan, before sitting down and pulling me on top of him.

We are still connected, him still half hard as he rubs my back and whispers in my ear, "I've missed you Fern. The sassy, smart-mouthed version."

I cry silent tears, because I've missed me, too. I missed enjoying sex and pleasure. I missed enjoying my fucking life.

His large hand wraps around the back of my head, tangling in my hair. His green eyes meet mine as he lifts my head, "Leave."

His eyes flicked toward one of the men closest to us. The man from the door I thought. I don't really care because Creed's eyes find mine again.

I hear them shuffle out of the room. The door clicking shut and Creed's mouth is on mine. His lips conquering, his tongue stroking the seam of my lips, asking for entry. I open for him, letting his breath become mine as all of the feelings

I have for him bubble up and out of me. I pour everything into this kiss as he holds me like a treasure.

His cock swells inside of me, already stiff for another round. This time he lets me control our pace. I roll my hips gently to match the sincerity of his kiss, and wrap my arms around his neck. We rock together, both our bodies speaking for us so we don't have to. I'm not ready for the conversation that this will lead to just yet.

His hands move down to grip my thighs as we grind against one another. Breaking the kiss he says, "You've always been mine Fern."

I still, letting that sink in, again. His eyes search mine, it isn't a question, because it's true.

I *have* always been his.

No matter how many times I tried to fuck him out of my system using someone else.

I nod, fresh tears trailing down my cheeks and he kisses them away.

Chapter Twenty-Nine

Creed cleans us up, rearranging my dress so I can pass as presentable after he just finished fucking me within an inch of my life. I stand, feeling his release shift inside of my body.

"That's inconvenient," I mutter.

"What?"

"Your cum is dripping out of me."

He grips my chin and kisses me, "Good."

I am going to be mortified if I sit down, sure that I will be sitting in a wet spot once this is over. The door to the room opens up and his family steps in.

Stopping in my tracks, I look to Creed who is standing with his legs apart and his fists clasped in front of his dick.

"Son," his father says, and hot damn, his voice is even deeper than Creed's.

"Father," Creed nods. "Mack."

I don't know if this is about to turn into a knock down drag out, or if they are always this... stern.

"Hi," I wave one hand, joining Creed where he stands, "I'm Fern."

They look me over, from my designer shoes to the roots of my raven hair. But I'm not about to start being insecure about the way I look. So I do the same, searching their faces and bodies.

Creed's brother has short hair cropped close to his scalp, where Creed has long wavy hair. His shoulders aren't as wide as Creed's and neither are their fathers. It's easy to see why Creed's father would choose him to take over.

"You've caused my family a great deal of trouble," their father finally speaks.

I'm unsure what he expects me to say, I am not sorry for his son choosing me. And I never will be.

"I've heard a lot about you too," I smile, testing his poker face.

He laughs then, it's a booming sort that I'm not convinced is completely jovial, "She reminds me of your mother."

I look at Creed, gauging his reaction. He loved his mother so much, so that has to be a complement. His lips tip up in a smile and I see his shoulders relax.

"I think you'll be well worth the trouble," his brother, Mack, says.

It is my turn to laugh, "I don't know about that."

"It takes a strong woman to be in your shoes," the way his father says it makes it feel like a warning.

"I think I can handle it," I grab Creed's forearm, anchoring myself.

They both smile and when I look at Creed, he is smiling too. They all hug then, all three smooshed into thick arms and when they release each other his father approaches me with his arms out.

I let him hug me, it's surprisingly sweet.

"Don't look so shocked," he shouts and laughs.

"I didn't expect you to be such a teddy bear."

They all laugh then, and Creed pulls me back into his side.

We eat a hot meal, as they ask me questions. His brother is hilarious, despite the way his face is set in a permanent scowl and the scar that runs over his right ear.

I watch them talk with a smile on my face, I can tell they share a special type of love. They have a bond that I will never have. It's peculiar, the way they speak as if there isn't a killer on the loose and they stepped into his territory.

All because Creed wants me safe. They came here when he called, dropped their whole lives to be here, for him and me.

"This guy," his father speaks. "He's killing your old lovers?"

I'm thrown off for a second, having to think back. Candy wasn't a lover, not really.

"It seems that way," I furrow my brows looking at Creed who doesn't look at all surprised about the connection. "I don't know why though."

"Pretty girl like you? Mayor's daughter, that's like royalty in this small town," Mack pipes up.

"Wait," I remember seeing something about kings and queens on the wall at Creeds, "Didn't the last poem have something about kings and queens in it?"

Creed puts his water back down and I nod, turning to face him fully.

"What if that's it? What if they think they have some sort of connection to my dad? Something with his campaign?"

"Your father has been the mayor for over twenty years," he reminds me.

"Right, but his benefactors are always changing. What if one of them thought I was also for sale, not like a donation, but as a pawn?"

"Your dad would never go for that," he shakes his head.

"Which would make whoever this person is, upset. Right?"

"Your wife may be on to something, have you checked his financials?" Mack asks. Their father is rubbing his beard, sitting back in the chair.

"I'll check it out," Creed promises, running a hand over my knee.

I can't let the thought go, I need to *know*. We are finally onto something, I can feel it. My phone rings, vibrating in my pocket. Candy's name flashing on the screen, along with her picture.

"Hello?" I answer, slipping out of the chair and striding over to near the window.

"Have you seen Manson?" she sounds panicked.

"Not since yesterday," I admit, "What's happened?"

I can hear her trying not to cry, the creek in her voice as she speaks, "He hasn't come back from your parent's, and it's almost dark."

She is scared, Manson has been at the hospital with her every night since the attack.

"I've tried calling him, texts, but it's like his phone is off," she hiccups."What if..."

"Don't finish that sentence," I warn.

I look back at the table and meet Creed's stare, "Have you called my mom? Dad?"

She sniffles and I hear the bed shift through the speaker, "No one is answering, I even called the house phone."

"Okay, I'm on my way."

Creed crosses the room in two strides, laying his hands on my shoulders, "Who was that?"

"Candy, she can't get anyone to answer their phone, and Manson isn't back at the hospital yet." I'm trying not to panic, not to jump to conclusions, "He wouldn't leave her alone there."

I click the screen on my phone hitting Manson's number, it doesn't even ring, just goes straight to voicemail. I look up at Creed and disconnect the call.

"Creed," I choke out and then dial my parents. I try calling my mother first because she always answers, but it rings, and rings.

Nothing.

I call dad next, praying that he will answer and tell me I am overreacting.

"We need to go," I storm to the door, angry tears blurring my vision.

"Whoa, Charmer," Creed's hand grabs onto my bicep, "Hold on."

His father and brother are already up and heading for the door with us, "We're here, son."

Creed looks at me, and licks his bottom lip, "Luca," he calls, "Start the cars, we need to get to the Hayes's now."

We rush out to the cars, Creed slamming the door behind

me and hopping in the drivers side, "Don't think the worst, okay baby?"

I nod as silent tears make their way down my cheeks.

The drive is faster than it should be, with Creed running near one hundred miles an hour. All three SUV's pull up to the house I grew up in, where four police cars are sitting in the drive with two ambulance's.

"No," I choke out.

I bolt from the car where Creed is yelling for me to wait.

I can't.

I can see the yellow tape on the doors, but I don't care. I throw myself inside.

Blood is everywhere, streaks running down the walls, splatters painting the ceilings as I walk through the foyer to the living room. I drop to my knees, sinking into the blood soaked carpet.

My parents are there, bodies prone and blue. When was the last time I spoke to them?

How can someone be this evil?

The fibers of the carpet squelch under my body as I crawl to them.

"Mom," I cry, feeling the tears drip onto the floor. Her arm is bent at an awkward angle, reaching for something. Her eyes closed, lips open, but she isn't breathing, "MOM!"

I scream, letting it ring out around the room.

"You can't be here!"

"This is a crime scene!"

Their protests fall on deaf ears, I hold her cold hand, and drape my body over hers, "Mommy."

I sob, my body shaking as I scream for someone to help her. No one comes, other than Creed. He kneels beside where I'm half on top of my mothers dead body, "Help her," I screech, "Please."

He runs a hand down my spine, shushing me as if I'm a child. She is dead, slaughtered in her own home.

"She's dead," I weep, "Creed."

I need him to fix her, to perform a miracle. Even though I know he can't.

"Charmer," he says after my body stops shaking, "Please, baby, come here."

With one last look at my mother, I crawl into Creed's lap and curl into a ball, "Is dad..."

Creed sweeps my hair from my face, and nods grimly. I don't need to ask anything else, my father is dead. Both of my parents, gone in a matter of days since I came home.

"I need you to leave," I say, trying to push myself out of his arms.

"We will."

"No, Creed, I need you to leave with them."

He looks down at me, face hard as steel, "If you aren't walking out that door, neither am I."

"Please," I place my hand on his cheek and swipe my thumb under his eye, "I can't lose anyone else."

"I'm not leaving you, end of story."

I wiggle out of his arms, standing up and walking to the door where Luca is waiting. I'm sure I look like a nightmare. Covered in blood that isn't my own, tears tracking over my cheeks.

He looks at me and places his fist over his heart, lifting it to his lips he kisses his knuckles and raises it up. I duck my head and try walking down the driveway, but Luca follows my every move.

My phone is vibrating in my pocket, I hadn't noticed it until now. I ignore it, I don't know if I can talk to anyone right now.

I walk and walk with Luca not so silently trailing after me. He is my shadow, the shadow I never asked for.

I just want to be alone.

Need to be alone.

Everyone I love is being murdered. Dropping like flies around a bug light. Every one of them, zapping as they die, that's how I feel. Like I'm being electrocuted every time someone dies.

I know it isn't my fault, I didn't ask anyone to do this. I loved my parents, I cared for Gray. I pull up the puzzle picture again, looking closer at it as if that might give me any memories.

Candy's face flashes on my screen, and I answer.

Manson is still missing.

"Candy." I hiccup.

"Oh thank God! Creed called, he sounded pissed. Manson just got here," she sighs and I hear muffled sobs, "he's not taking the news well."

"How is he supposed to act?" I snap.

"I just wanted you to know your brother is safe," she whispers and I immediately feel bad, truly, "And that Dean and Gretchen were trying to get into my room when he got here."

"Why?" I stop walking, behind me I hear Luca unholster his glock.

Spinning around I shake my head, there is no danger, not here at least.

"Gretchen wanted to check on me, and well since her and Dean got engaged..."

He's always around more, I can hear what she isn't saying. Gretchen is okay, I have to remember that we aren't teenagers anymore.

"Can I talk to Manson?"

"Ferny," his voice sounds broken, low and soft, "What are we going to do?"

"I don't know," I cry too, joining him in his grief for our parents, "Can I come there?"

"Where's Creed?"

The mention of his name is like an arrow being shot into my chest. I left him with my parents dead bodies and the police. He will take care of everything, it's his way, but I should be with him.

"He's still in the house," I start back from the way I came, "I had to get out."

"Listen, Ferny. I love you, but you can't push any of us away now," I can hear the tears in his voice, "We need you, and Creed won't admit it, but it will destroy him if you walk away from him now."

He's right, but I can't lose anyone else.

Because that will destroy *me*.

Chapter Thirty

I walk back to the house, Luca still on my heels, but he hasn't said anything as I retrace my path back. The silence of the night is unnerving, as if the very world is holding its breath.

A part of me wants to be dead too, the same part that I thought had healed.

"Your brother is right," Luca says, falling into step beside me, "Boss would tear apart the world for you, if only you asked."

"How long have you known him?"

"Since before he was who he is now," his stare is straight ahead, but his words hit me square in the stomach, "I've known about you, too."

"Me?" I can't picture Creed as a 'gossip about my feelings' type.

Luca stops me with a gentle hand on my shoulder. "He's going to kill me for telling you this, but that man has been in love with you for a long damn time."

I know he loves me, it's in all the things he has done since I came home. It's in the way he holds me while we sleep. I can't walk away from him, even if I want to.

Even though I probably should.

We stand there for a few minutes, Luca lets me collect myself without judgment. When I am ready, we start again, this time our steps a little faster, and when we get back within sight of the house I run.

Creed stands on the steps, arms crossed over his chest speaking to the coroner. His head swivels to where I'm running and he meets me on the bottom stair.

I breathe him in as I crash into him, the smell of his cologne, the way his heart pounds behind his ribs. He's *alive*, and he's *here*.

His hand moves behind my head as he holds me against him. The other lifts me up under my bottom. My legs circle his waist and I cry. He stands there with me in his arms, whispering comforting words as I let it all out.

I lift my head when I hear the gurney's being wheeled out, I'm not sure why. Maybe morbid curiosity, or closure, I honestly don't know.

"Look at me baby," he whispers, "You've been through enough tonight."

Our eyes clash like two magnets, "I'm sorry for running off."

He doesn't yell at me, or tell me how stupid it was, had Luca not been here. He simply kisses my temple and sets me on my feet, "We'll head home in a few, for now will you wait in the car?"

I look up at the home I've made so many memories in, and let it go. I will always remember the good, but the bad has a tendency to linger. I'm ready to grieve my parents, find this monster to put an end to his terror, and live.

"Promise we'll get him?"

"If it's the last fucking thing I do," he vows.

Luca walks me to the car, and I lay down on the backseat letting myself feel everything at once. I scream into the leather, until I'm horse.

When Creed opens the door, he pulls me up and I pound my fists on his chest. Screaming at him, at the world.

"Why?" I sob, knees giving out, landing in the pebbles of the driveway. Creed follows me down, scooping me up and holding me as I fold my fists into his shirt. Letting my tears and snot mix on the material.

I heave and my breaths get stuck in my chest. He rubs my back, letting me get everything out.

I don't remember falling asleep, until Creed shifts me out

of the car and I rouse.

He adjusts my body in his arms—one arm supporting my back, the other under my knees—and carries me into the house. It's too quiet, I have a feeling Luca, Diego, and Nile have something to do with that.

Up the stairs we go, he doesn't falter as we make it through the door heading straight for the bathroom. He peels my dress off my body, kissing me deeply piece by piece. I know what he's doing, keeping me in the moment before getting rid of the last of my soiled clothes.

When I'm naked, he walks me to the bathtub where he pours in lavender oils and salts. I climb in and sit with my knees to my chest as the water fills.

He stays with me, washing my hair and body with the utmost care. We don't speak, no words are needed as the water surrounds my body, leaving droplets like diamonds on my skin.

When he is done, he drains the tub. I watch as the water swirls and mixes with my mothers blood. On autopilot I stand and he wraps me in a towel, lifting me out of the tub and gently placing me on the counter.

"Bear with me, baby, I've never done this before."

His tattooed hands pick my witch hazel bottle out of my products and pours it on a cotton pad. Lifting it to my skin, he runs the cool agent over my cheeks, chin, and forehead.

The smell brings me comfort, it's a routine I never forget. Something my mother taught me a long time ago.

Next, he looks between the moisturizer and serum drops. His eyes go to the other side, and I decide to take pity on him.

"The blue one," my voice is small, but he hears me all the same.

He dabs a bit of the cream out of the jar and softly brushes it on my face and neck. When he's finished, he lifts my body butter and starts to slather it on my shoulders. I let the towel fall as he takes his time working the citrus scented lotion into my skin.

When he's satisfied with his work, he helps me into bed. Crawling in behind me after a quick shower himself, he knots our bodies together.

His lips brush my jaw as my eyes blink heavily, "Sleep Charmer, you're safe."

Those are the last words I hear before falling into a dreamless sleep.

The next few days are a whirlwind of questions, sitting in the planning room, and keeping enough food down so that Creed won't complain. I know he's concerned, and he has every reason to be.

I have a bad history with death.

We still aren't any closer to finding out who is doing all of this, and it's starting to drive me bonkers.

Luca, Nile, and Diego take turns watching me at the barn. I named Daisy's little boy, Rambow, he's rambunctious and a little clumsy. He is fun to watch trying to intimidate his mama. When I saddle Daisy for the first time here, I take the time to let her get used to the new outfit. The blanket alone is so much nicer than anything at the ranch, and the saddle is tanned leather, emblazoned with my nickname.

It's the first thing that made me laugh in those first few days after I found my parents murdered. I can't look at the media fearing I'll see my fathers face. Press conferences and an interim mayor have to be chosen.

Daisy takes right to the new equipment, letting me ride for a few hours each day. I take her over the crests and valleys of the land Creed and Manson share, and return before sundown.

I'm just walking into the house when I hear one of the boys yelling.

"You will go," Nile's distinct Italian accent floats through the room, "And that's the last I'll hear about it."

Fuck, I wouldn't want to be on the receiving end of that.

I hightail it up to my room, where Creed is sitting in his black and white tux, waiting for me.

He looks at his watch, "Cutting it close, Charmer."

I look at the clock on the wall. I have thirty minutes before we need to leave. To be honest, I am putting it off until the last minute. I'm not ready to bury my parents, and Candy was just released from the hospital yesterday.

She has been resting and taking it easy. Manson won't let her out of his sight, and I can't blame him, I would do the same with Creed.

"Go shower," he commands, pulling me from my thought spiral.

I do, showering quickly and drying my hair. He is on the phone, I can hear him grunt through the door every time I pause the dryer to brush my tangles.

Someone must have bought me a new black dress. The one I assume I'm supposed to wear is hanging up in the middle of the closet. It's simple, just a black dress that is snug around my thighs and waist.

The entire dress is covered in black lace, billowy and sleeved. New black heels sit below where the dress hangs and I wonder if Creed picked this out, or if he has a personal shopper.

It doesn't matter, I need to put the dress on and suffer through a whole crowd of people wanting to offer Manson and I their condolences.

Slipping the dress over my hips, I zip the small zipper in the back and bend to work my feet into the heels. Creed's shiny black shoes come into view and I stand up, understandably jumpy.

He crosses the space between us and lifts my chin with two fingers, "I'll be with you all night."

I nod and kiss him, thanking him with my love rather than words.

He walks with me, hand on the small of my back as we make our way downstairs. Luca, Nile, Diego, and the boys are all dressed in a full tuxedo. Ranging from black on black, to black and white, to gray.

Tearing up at all of them, I nod, acknowledging their support. The boys have been the most surprising group. The four of them are thick as thieves, two of them turned out to be twins. They offered to teach me their video games, take me to the shooting range, or go out and get me whatever chocolate I wanted.

I declined all of their offers, but stuck around while they

played their games. I learned a lot from them while they didn't know I was paying attention. They love Creed in a way I can't put into words.

Which now extends to me, I just hope I'm worthy of it.

Toby and Talon, the twins, step forward and hug me. It still surprises me that they are only seventeen. Banks settles his hand on my shoulder, and Henry grips my hand. It's sweet, and exactly what I need.

"We will all be there tonight, if you need to get away, even just to breathe, one of us will be with you," Creed whispers in my ear, "You're not alone."

I take a deep breath and shake my head, "Let's go then."

Chapter Thirty-One

We all pile into three SUV's. Creed drives the two of us alone, Diego drives one with Henry and Banks, and Luca and Nile drive with the twins and Mack. City Hall is exactly the same as it had been when I last visited.

The gray stone of the building is cracked in some places, plastered together in others, but it's my dads legacy. He loved being the Mayor of Gravity Hill. The office staff has a spread of cheese and meats along with punch and water in the center of the entryway.

Pictures of my parents are on easels that dot the room. I spot Manson and Candy, already in the back room speaking to some of the staff here in City Hall.

I tug Creed in that direction and everyone breaks off into pairs. I'm sure we look like a formidable bunch. With nine men flanking me during our entrance. Maybe that's what Creed wants, to make it clear no one can fuck with us.

Creed's father is here, along with his brother. It isn't the first time I have seen them since our initial meeting, but it seems like it when they kiss each of my cheeks and tell me, again, how sorry they are.

They don't need me to speak, they just hover near where Manson and Candy are. I wonder if Creed had them come too, just in case the murderer decides to show up. I have been wracking my brain trying to figure out who is in the puzzle picture with me.

I even made a list in my journal of all the people I can remember hooking up with in a truck bed. It's a small list, and only two are unharmed currently, that we knew of.

"Oh Fern," Mrs. Doben says, pulling me from my thoughts, "I'm so sorry."

I accept her hug, only wrapping one of my arms around her. I still have Creed's hand firmly tangled in mine. If I'm his lighthouse, he's my anchor.

"Thank you Mrs. Doben," I don't really know what else to say, so we stand there in silence until more people who knew my parents come through the receiving line. I'm getting tired of hearing how *sorry* people are.

I turn after the most recent line has a gap, clutching Creed's arm and tugging him with me through a hallway that is blocked off for tonight. I lead him through the hall into my father's private office.

The door still squeaks when I push it open, and I smile, knowing how much that entertained him. Pulling Creed into the room and shutting the door I let out a sigh and fall into one of the leather chairs across from my dads old desk.

I rub circles on my temples while Creed crouches down and rubs my thighs.

"When you're ready, we can go," he's being gentle with me.

I shake my head, "I can't leave Manson, plus Candy is still recovering."

He doesn't say anything, or offer to leave again. I look around the office, noting the pictures of all four of my family members in golden frames. Someone will have to take those down. Along with his newspaper clippings and degrees.

A knock sounds on the door before it opens. Manson stands there, leaning against the frame, taking it all in.

"Strange to see it without him in it," he crosses his arms over his chest. "He had such a big presence."

I nod, I don't disagree, our father was as loyal and joyous as they come. He really cared about Gravity Hill, how could someone rip him from this world so cruelly? Creed stands, extending his hand to me and I take it.

He pulls me up, and we follow Manson out. Candy comes out of the bathroom across the hall and wraps me in a hug.

I was nervous to hug her, I didn't want to rip open any stitches.

"Can I have a minute?" I ask Creed and Manson, I need to cry with my best friend. To tell her what is going on in my head. Creed kisses my temple and walks back toward the room where people are waiting to speak to us and Manson trails after him.

I hold Candy, swaying to music that isn't there. She let's me cry into her shirt while I catch her up on everything we have put together.

She takes a deep breath and lets it out, "God Fern, why would they do this?"

"I wish I knew," I shake my head and let my arms fall, "Why me? There's nothing special about me."

"I don't think what's happening has to do with how special you think you are," she runs her hand over my arm and squeezes my wrist, "Take a minute, all these kiss-asses can wait."

I laugh and turn to walk into the women's bathroom. It's small, with only two stalls, but it is private. After sitting on the toilet to gather myself I walk out of a stall and nearly scream.

Dean is standing at the door, arms crossed, smirking, "Sorry."

He scared the shit out of me and all he has to say is sorry? Not only that but he is in a private bathroom, for women.

"You need to leave," I'm not in the mood for a verbal sparring match.

"I have a few questions, Fern," he croons, raising his hands as if that will make me feel safe.

"You can ask them in the lobby, where everyone else is."

"I don't think I can," he chuckles, "Because that big brute of a *husband* of yours is always around."

He put quotations and extra emphasis around the word husband. I'm not sure how to take that, yeah, I don't wear a ring, but neither does Creed. It doesn't mean we aren't married, or in love.

"I can see those wheels spinning behind your eyes,. Dean steps closer, "Why is it that the moment you come back, you're married?"

His eyes are bloodshot, he is rolling on something.

"Tell me, did you say 'I do', before or after Gray's blood dried?"

"You need to back the fuck up, Dean," I will not step back, no matter how much I want to, "I'm leaving, and you're going to let me."

His casual mention of that night strikes a bolt of fear straight to my stomach. Why is he bringing up Gray's name at all?

He places a hand on his chest and sweeps his other arm out toward the door, "I'll be seeing you."

It's creepy and cryptic as fuck, I can hear his laugh even after the door closes. I hustle back to the lobby where Creed immediately pulls me into his side, "What's wrong?"

I must look panicked, "Dean cornered me in the bathroom."

"He what?" he roars. "Did he touch you?"

I shake my head, "he brought up Gray, said I married you before his blood was cold."

He runs a hand over his hair and the other balls into a fist, "Where is he?"

"Not here," I whisper, I can see the curious looks he is accruing, "I left him in the bathroom."

He tugs me toward Manson, "We need to wrap this up."

Manson takes one look at Creed and tells Mrs. Doben that it's time we left, that Candy isn't feeling well. She tells us she will clean up, practically shooing us out the door.

Creed whistles and it seems like all the men melt out of the shadows. They're there so fast I have to blink a few times to make sure I'm not imagining things.

"Boss?" Luca nods toward a truck that is driving slowly by.

It's navy.

"The picture," I whisper. "It was Dean."

Everyone's eyes land on me, and I sense the heat that covers my face. That night in the picture was the first night I hooked up with Dean, it was ages ago. I don't remember him taking a picture. If I would have known, I would have made him delete it.

"We need to head home," Manson holds Candy who is leaning on him heavily.

Mack offers to help Manson get Candy into the car, and the rest of us climb into our SUV's.

"Wait, your dad," I lay my hand on his arm, scanning the parking lot.

"I'll call him," Creed hits a button on his steering wheel and tells the automaton to call Hemlock. I lower one brow, he calls his dad Hemlock?

I don't even think it rings before he picks up and Creed tells him to meet us at the house.

There is something on his mind, I can tell by the way he's working his jaw with the hand he isn't using to drive.

"Tell me," I tilt my head, looking at his profile in the street lights.

"Something you said, about Dean."

I groan, and he shoots me a dark look.

"Not about hooking up with him," he swats my leg, "You

said he asked if we were married before *Gray's* blood was cold."

Before he finishes everything clicks.

Dean is the murderer.

Gray wasn't his legal name, and that isn't what the press published. How would Dean have known the nickname I gave him, unless he had been stalking me...or there that night.

"Oh God," I start to hyperventilate, "he said he'd be seeing me."

Creed pulls the SUV over and kills the engine, "If he is the one doing all of this, we have an army at our back," his hands clutches the sides of my face, "And I'll be damned if I let anyone else you love die."

He takes deep breaths with me, calming my racing heart and quelling my anxiety. When he is content that I'm okay he cranks the car back onto the road, and drives the rest of the way home.

"We know who's behind all of this," Creed starts, addressing the room full with the boys, his men, dad, and brother, "His name is Dean Smith."

"So what are we going to do about it?" His father asks, voice booming.

"We're going to take him off the fucking board," Creed

growls, "I'm going to take every pound of flesh that motherfucker has earned."

"We're with you," his brother stands, "And we can call in the others."

Creed shakes his head, "He outed himself during the funeral to Fern, so he may know we're coming."

"We need to make a plan," Nile says, "And contingencies."

They all murmur their agreement, and start talking over each other. It goes on like that for a few hours.

By the time everyone is satisfied with the plan it's past midnight. I checked on Manson and Candy before they settled in, and at some point I dozed off, even amongst all the deep timbres and shouts.

When I crack my eyes open it's dark, but I'm in the bedroom, with Creed snuggled around my body. His soft snores tickle my ears and then I remember everything from tonight.

Untangling myself from his embrace I wrap up in a robe from the closet and sit in the sitting room. A combination of emotions seizes me.

Pissed, terrified, sad, even a little relief. I need to journal. I haven't done it in a while, and my fingers are itching to write.

Processing my feelings got easier when I started writing

them, now it's the only way I can separate and heal those parts.

I am so busy scratching away on my paper that I don't hear Creed arrive. He stands in the doorway with only boxers on, hands grabbing the arch above him and leaning in. His torso stretches like a lazy cat in the sun, and my God, I want to lick every inch of him.

Swiping my bottom lip with my tongue I smile, teeth stuck on my bottom lip.

"You're journaling?" He asks, nodding to the book filled with my inner thoughts.

"Couldn't sleep," it's not totally untrue, I had fallen asleep, but the nightmares have returned.

He cuts across the space, pulling me up into his arms and plopping us back down on the couch so his legs bracket my body, and my back is to his chest.

"Do you want to talk about it?" He offers, and I find that I do. I want to tell him about the nightmares from that night, and the way my feelings cross and tangle. I talk, and ramble about everything.

He leans back, circling his arms around me as I read what I wrote. We talk about the nightmares and he helps me come to terms with what happened. It's cathartic and wholesome.

Everything I didn't know how to ask for, and he offered it

freely.

I yawn and shut my journal, feeling lighter than I have in a long time. Creed carries me to bed and peppers my skin with kisses until I fall asleep.

Manson and Candy come over the next morning, and lord have mercy, turns out we do need the table that sits thirty people. The dining room is full to the brim with huge men who look like they could kill with their bare hands.

The boys; Henry, Talon, Toby, and Banks line one side of the table, and along the other side sits Nile, Diego, Luca, and Creed's father and brother.

It's...overwhelming in the best way. Our home is full of people who care, mostly. Some I can tell are just excited for the torture.

The whole house feels loud, and I love it. I enjoy listening to everyone chat and bicker about different things, watching them all with a small smile.

"Hello, wife," Creed speaks low in my ear, he pulled Manson and Candy into the clue room and told them everything earlier. It must have gone well, based on the way Manson is smiling and Candy nods her head toward me giving me a small reassuring grin.

He places his hands on my shoulders and squeezes. I am sitting at the head of the table, where they all demanded I sit.

"Hello, husband," my smile spreads, splitting my face in two. I turn around to face him, earning a kiss, and some toast thrown at my head.

"Talon," Creed warns.

"How did you know?" I chuckle.

"He's the only fucker at the table with the balls to do it," his eyes cut to where Talon sits and I laugh at the sheer force he is.

"We're gonna have to do something about that," I tease.

Even though we have all of this shit going on, it's nice to sit down and enjoy the company for a moment. No matter how long it lasts.

Chapter Thirty-Two

The house is full, and even though it's because there's a murderer we're hunting down, it feels wholesome. It's hard to describe as I doodle in my journal, while the men make plans and run through scenarios.

Talon plops down on to the couch beside me, controller in hand. The rest of the boys are touring a school that will allow them to transfer in at the start of their senior year. It's what he and his father, Nile, had been arguing over a few days ago when I accidentally walked in on them.

"Too cool for school?" Sarcasm coats my tongue.

Talon's ocean eyes slide to the side, "So original, step-mommy."

"Step-mommy?" I raise my brows, "What an honor, and here I thought you didn't particularly care for me."

He chuckles darkly, "Oh, I don't."

I readjust my journal, flipping the pages over so it's covered. Shifting to stand, Talon's hand whips out and lands softly on my arm.

"But," he says as I turn to find his eyes trained on mine, "Creed loves you, and I love that bastard... so how can I make you feel better?"

I'm taken back, *Talon* is the one asking how to make me feel better. I debate fucking with him to see how far I can push him, but the way his face is pinched, tells me it took a lot for him to ask.

"While I appreciate that you care so much for Creed, I don't think there's much anyone can do for me."

Shrugging away from his hand, I head to the kitchen. Talon follows, hanging sideways off the door molding.

"Nothing?" he prompts, "Not even say... a jaguar?"

I spin around, nearly dropping the glass I pulled from the cabinet.

"Come again?" I ask, trying to mask my smile, because Creed did *not* tell them about my ridiculous thoughts.

Talon laughs, placing one hand on his stomach, "That was too good, really. A fucking mascot? Were you high that night?"

"For your information, I wasn't born into this world, it was a perfectly valid question!" I defend, realizing this conversation for what it is, a distraction. Something to lift a bit of the heaviness, I just didn't think–in a million eons–that the one executing said plan would be Talon.

His whole, grumpy assholery vibe doesn't really make him the captain of the sunshine committee.

"Sure it was," he nods, stepping up to me and taking the glass from my hands. He adds the small cubes of ice I like into the glass and places it under the filter. I watch him, as he watches the glass fill.

He hands it to me after he's satisfied with the amount of liquid to ice ratio.

"Thanks," my voice lifts a little, because this isn't the same Talon I've come to know. "Uhm, is there something I'm missing?" I ask as I take a sip of the water.

Talon hops up onto the bar, sitting there like a little shit who knows Creed will lose his mind if he finds his ass on the counter.

"I don't hate you," he starts and rolls his eyes at my smile, "You aren't *terrible*," he corrects.

"Mhmm," I murmur as I take another sip.

"Home has meant a lot of different things to us. Toby, Henry, and Banks, and me. It's been a long time since we've had any sort of female relationship that wasn't just to get laid."

My face scrunches in distaste, and confusion as he continues.

"I've never really been good at letting people come into our lives, but Creed... he's the best of us, even in his worst times. And he's been obsessed with you for as long as I can remember. So, maybe I'm not the cover model for 'welcoming weekly', but I'd like to try."

I could tell it took a lot for him to admit even one of those sentences, but he was trying, and I remember Creed telling me their mother just walked out, how could I deny him my best effort to be a role model. Maybe not a mother, but something akin to it.

"As long as you stop calling me step-mommy, I'd like to get to know the four of you better," I announce.

He chuckles and hops down from the counter, patting my shoulder, "Oh no, mommy dearest, I think the nick-name stays." I shake my head as he walks back out to the living room shouting over his shoulder, "Come on, step-mommy, let me show you how to play, so I can kick your ass virtually."

Shaking with laughter I join him, allowing him to teach me about their games, and watching him ease out of his protective bubble. After a few games I yawn and lay down, resting my feet near Talon's legs.

"I'll go to the school, if the rest of them like it," he whispers. "On the condition that we can come home whenever we want."

"I don't think I get to make those conditions, Talon." I tell him while my eyes drift shut.

"No, but I think our dads will listen if you agree with me."

I crack an eye open and smirk, "That's it isn't it? Your angle."

He rolls his eyes and lays his head back on the couch, "I'm serious."

"I know you are, I have a feeling if you ask, your fathers will be more than happy to have your back... within reason."

"Now you sound like Creed," he scoffs and I laugh, because fuck me, I sure do.

Creed wakes me up from my nap with kisses on my temple. We all eat dinner together and when everyone is full, leaning back in their seats, Creed begins going over the final plan to trap Dean and bring him to my parents house.

It's currently empty, and the police already swept it. The perfect place to have him admit his crimes.

I just need to play my part.

Chapter Thirty-Three

reed, Manson, and the rest of the guys roll out the next day. I kissed Creed this morning long and slow, after he made love to me. If the plan goes sideways he will most likely be the next person on Dean's list.

He promised he won't do anything heroic though, nothing to make himself an easy target. Manson is with him and he won't let him do anything stupid.

Plus, I have a feeling in my gut that Nile, Diego, and Luca would take a bullet for Creed.

Creed's dad and brother stay with me and Candy at the house. I got to know them better, and it's nice in a scary way. They tell me stories of Creed when he was younger, embarrassing things that I will most definitely be using in a fight.

When I start to get antsy waiting by the phone, Creed's brother, Mack, walks Candy and I out to the barn where I introduce them to Daisy.

She is happy to see me, though Rambow is not. He nudges Mack with his head any time he gets close to Daisy.

It's adorable, and the look on his face every time Rambow does it is priceless.

Hours run down to minutes, and I start to worry.

"The plan will work, Fern," his brother says, noting my anxiety, "Give them faith."

I nod, waiting for the moment my phone will ring, and I can *do* something. Waiting around is suffocating and pokes holes in my confidence. We watch Daisy and Rambow walk the ring, heads nodding with every step.

The sun starts setting, so I feed them some carrots and lead them back to their stall. Soon he will need his own, and have to be separate from his mom. But for tonight he will get to stay. I make sure their stall is mucked out before I walk back with Mack and Candy.

Conall lifts his head from where he had it leaned back on the couch, "How are the ponies?"

"They're good," I chuckle, knowing how much he hates horses. He's trying to distract me, and I appreciate the attempt.

Candy turns on the TV that is usually used for video games. Honestly, I don't even know if it works with normal channels and movies. Creed and I usually don't stick around when the boys play.

We escape to the barn or our room most of the time, talking and spending every minute we can together.

Candy chooses a baking show, and lets it play. I didn't realize all the shit you can do with sweets. These contestants are talking about flavor combinations and doing all kinds of things to their cakes. I almost forget about the phone call I'm waiting on.

Until my phone rings.

An unknown number, like we knew it would be. Creed's Dad, Mack, and Candy all watch the screen as I hit the answer button.

"Hello?"

"It's about time you answered one of my calls, my fire," his voice is screened with a modulator, making his voice sound almost robotic. The way he calls me 'my fire' makes me want to retch, but I agreed that I could do this.

"Who is this?" I'm supposed to play dumb, like I didn't know he would be calling. Like I don't know who he is.

"I thought you'd have figured it out by now," he tisks. "You used to be so smart."

I don't know how to answer that, my eyes widen as I start to panic, what am I supposed to say? Conall puts his hand on my knee and mouths 'wait'. I do, letting the silence grow between us.

I hear a deep sigh from the phone, "Honestly, I'm disappointed. But, not to worry, I have your last surprise right here."

Muffled voices come from the speakers and my heart plummets.

"If another dead body is the surprise, I don't want it," I cup my phone in my hands, wishing I could see through it.

He laughs, a manic type sound that gives me chills, "I did some research first, my little fire, turns out you really are married to this raging asshole who took advantage of my night."

Grumbles and scuffling sounds come from the speakers and I look around the room, "Please don't hurt him, Dean."

Conall looks at me curiously, I'm not following the plan. But neither is Dean, and I can't live with myself if I don't try to save Creed.

"Ah, my love, you've finally caught on. Why would you marry him when he hurt you? All those years, embarrassing yourself pining over him," he scoffs, "and for what?"

"Please," I'll beg, if that's what he wants in exchange for Creed's life, I will get on my knees and plead, "Tell me what you want."

"I want you."

"Done," I don't hesitate, "When and where?"

Again that manic laugh filters through the phone, "You can only save one though, who will it be? I'll be waiting where the moonlight first touched us. Tonight."

The line goes dead, "We need a new plan."

Creed's father is already on the phone, barking orders and questions into the mouthpiece. Mack is doing the same, standing up and going outside.

Candy's face has gone pale as she stares at her phone.

"Candy?"

"He has Manson too," she whispers, turning her head to face me, "He's going to kill one of them."

"No he won't," Conall declares. "He won't be killing either of them."

The sliding door opens and Mack walks in, "We have a new plan."

Luca and Nile burst in, carrying a limp Diego, breaths puffing from exhaustion. I'm floored at the view, he's bloody and bruised. Mack jumps in to help at the sight, they place him on the couch and I hold Candy's hand.

"He'll be okay," Luca voices noting my horror, "Fucker ran over him with the car."

"His car?" I screech, what the hell did I get them into?

"I'll call Gran," Mack pauses to look at his father, "Unless you have someone else in mind."

Creed's dad looks at Mack, silently communicating to each other in a language they know well. Conall turns after Mack nods in agreement to look at Diego and shakes his head, "Send the jet for her."

"Wait," I throw out my hands, "We still need a plan!"

"We're going to that meeting," Conall voices, "And you're going to put on the best acting performance of your life, because it's got to feel real for you, Fern. I won't tell you the details and have you giving us away."

That's fair, not very nice, but fair.

"Okay," I turn to look at Candy, "Can you show them where to go?"

She nods, features determined.

I kiss her cheek and take off toward the garage.

"For fuck sakes Fern," Conall stops me in my tracks, "Give us a few minutes before you just take off."

I do as he asks, legs bouncing in Creed's SUV. When Candy texts me the go ahead, I punch the door opener and hit the gas. I'm praying the whole way there, that Creed's family knows what they're doing.

The night is dark, save for the moon that shines like a beacon. I break about four laws getting here, but when I do I rush out of Creed's SUV, and run to where the two of them are bound, only to be caught around the middle by arms that have given me nightmares for years. I may not have known who it was, but I remember the feeling of his hands in my hair. I'll never forget.

"You're so *predictable*, my fire," Dean's slimy voice is in my ear, his breath hot against the side of my face and I want to vomit on his shoes.

I can feel the sheer confidence in Dean, the way he feels like he has already won, vibrating under his skin. I push him away, dragging my eyes to the two people I love most in the world.

Creed and Manson are on their knees. Creed has a cut on his neck that is steadily trickling down to his shirt, and Manson looks worse for wear, my heart beats in relief.

At least they're both still alive.

Manson's brown hair is disheveled, his skin is dirty, and he has a bruise on his cheek that looks like it hurts. Dean's arms wind around my neck, crossing and squeezing. I cough as he keeps me there.

Anger simmers under my skin and I tear myself out of Dean's arms.

"You're a fucking monster," I wail, my voice cracking with unshed tears, "Leave them out of this fantasy of yours."

"My fire, you don't understand," he grips my hands, "But

you will, you'll see everything I did was for you. For *us*."

His eyes are bloodshot, and wild. Darting from their faces and back to me. He licks his lips, and dives in for a kiss. I jerk away, but his hands hold firm.

"Let go of me!"

Instead of pulling me in, he shoves me to the gravel, and turns toward the two men I have left in my life who mean the most to me.

"It's only fitting that we're all back here," Dean raises his voice, "Where it all started. Where the beginning of our beautiful life blossomed."

The only thing I know for sure happened here is Gray's murder, and the site where I would have become a missing person.

Something like hurt flashes across Dean's face before it's gone in a blink. He is acting strange, muttering to himself and getting visibly irritated.

"I guess I can't expect you to remember, after all the whoring around you did," he hangs his head as if he's disappointed, "You should have just stayed with me, Fern. I could have made you happy."

"Dean, please," I sob, "Let them go."

He tuts, and spins around to crouch down in front of me.

"This is where we lost our virginities, you and I," his hand cups my chin, fingers digging into my flesh, "And you don't even remember."

His words paint a picture in my mind, the same picture the puzzle finally made. Me, in pink lingerie, lounged out in the back of a truck. I don't remember that night because it was just another night of debauchery for me. God, we were *kids*. It's been a decade since then.

I had just turned eighteen, and Dean was *there*, it didn't mean anything to me, and it most definitely wasn't my first time.

A little laugh escapes me, a deranged sort that doesn't match the gravity of the situation, he's hung up on a legitimate fantasy. "I wasn't a virgin." I spit, hoping he will end this nightmare, or focus on me.

His eyes darken, and I immediately realize my mistake. He shoots up, striding to where Creed is kneeling tall.

"No, no, no, no!" Dean pleads, "You're lying, just like you did when you told me you'd see me again. All these years I've waited patiently, and you marry *him*?"

Dean flashes the knife, holding it against Creed's neck where fresh blood blooms and spills over the blade. For his part, Creed doesn't make a sound.

"Stop!" I screech, "Dean, please, why? It's been years."

He's no longer listening to me though, lost in whatever

thoughts are plaguing him. Murmuring to himself, talking rapidly and I can't understand. I can't keep up with his ramblings.

"Dean," I shout, getting my feet under me and walking closer.

"Don't," Dean snarls, spit flies my way and I stop my steps. He is digging the knife in farther, I can see where the indent is pressing the sharp blade into Creed's neck and I want to do anything, *anything* to make that knife disappear.

"Okay, put the knife down, please. You're scaring me."

I don't know if it's enough to get him away from Creed, but I have to try, before he kills the man I love.

His hand lowers and his eyes turn pitying, "My fire."

I cringe, wishing he would stop calling me that. I am not his anything, I belong to one man, and he is currently on his knees, bound, with a knife to his throat. From where Dean threw me to the ground, I can see Nile on his stomach in the grass, inching closer with every second.

Trying not to look at him and give him away, I swivel to Dean.

I don't know what the plan will be once Nile gets them free, it is clear Dean is high on something stronger than ibuprofen, and I don't want anyone dying tonight.

He swings the knife around, pointing it in my direction

before speaking.

"Your heart is so big, even for these two, who betrayed you, and left you alone in that barn!"

"I know, but I've forgiven them, maybe I can forgive you too," I'm hoping for a hail mary at this point, Dean's hands fall to his sides and he moves over to me. Gathering me in his arms as he sighs.

"They all have to die, my fire. For us to be happy, they have to pay for their wrongs against you."

"And what about my parents?" I'm crying now, tears drip down my cheeks as I think about the two people who didn't deserve his delusion, "Why did they have to die?"

His face twists in disgust, and he spits on the ground, "Your parents are the worst kind of monsters, Fern. They allowed this criminal to marry you, without your *consent*."

He goes to turn away from me and I wrap my arms around him. I hate the feeling of his body touching mine, the wrongness of it but I need to keep him occupied. He raises his hand to wipe the tears off my face, "I made it right, for you."

I hiccup, choking on another sob, and willing my body to relax. As much as I don't want him anywhere near me, I know Nile needs a few more seconds.

I can give that to him.

"You don't have to watch, I can take care of it, for the both of us," he tips my head back and I freeze. His face was twisted into a sick smile, as if he enjoys all of the killing he's done.

"You killed that woman too, didn't you. The one the police thought I killed."

His tongue darts over his top lip and he frowns, "That was an accident, unfortunate for her, but she got in my way. I almost had you, Fern, and she kept pestering me after I'd lost you in the woods. I had to do it, so I could focus on finding you. I didn't mean to hurt you, you have to know that."

"I picked your keys up, because you ran away from me. I was there to *save* you, and you ran. I stabbed her with your keys, right in the neck. She was going to hurt you, calling you awful names. I couldn't let her get away with that."

He runs a hand over my hair, and kisses the top of my head.

"She didn't deserve to die, Dean."

Nile has managed to get Creed un-tied as well as Manson. Together they help Manson up and I notice the awkward way his foot sways as he limps toward the ditch.

Dean is rambling now, full shouts that sound a lot like poetry. He turns, eyes landing on Creed who is turned around helping Nile get Manson away from Dean.

Dean starts toward him, holding the knife high above his shoulder.

"Behind you!" I howl, as loud as I can. My voice cracks like a whip through the forest.

Dean brings the knife down just as Creed throws up his arm. Bright red blood flows from where Dean manages to clip him.

I'm frozen, watching Creed grip Dean's wrist, wrestling the knife from his hand. But Dean either isn't affected by the pain, or he simply doesn't care.

He snaps and snarls at Creed as the woods illuminate and men that I recognize from the restaurant appear. They don't hesitate to help Creed as Luca runs to me, pulling me away from the frenzy. Dean is fighting tooth and nail, all while screaming that he was helping me.

That he is who I need.

It takes five men to haul him to the ground, and he doesn't go without head butting the man with the bubbly scar, "Fucking asshole," he rubs the spot after they've tied Dean up with rope and zip ties.

Creed rushes to me once Dean is hauled away, enveloping me in his arms and crushing me to his chest.

"Don't you ever do anything like that again," he reprimands, taking my face in his hands and mashing his lips against mine. We embrace each other, letting the moment sink in.

He is hurt, but alive.

"We're going to take this piece of scum now, boss," Luca stands near a van I hadn't seen come up the road. I'm assuming they put Dean inside it, but I wasn't paying attention, and I also don't care.

Creed nods and shifts so I can see Mack helping Manson into another car where Candy is waiting. He nods and says, "Gran."

Creed groans, but doesn't say anything else.

"Who is Gran?"

"She's going to love you," he kisses my nose, "Let's just say, she's our doctor."

I can't get into anything else, my brain is already on overload. He helps me into the car, and we head back to the place I thought I'd never want to go back to.

The house looks the same, lacking in its luster because I know my parents aren't behind that door anymore. But maybe witnessing this will help, in some fucked up way. Watching Dean pay for all the things he has done could help me find peace.

"You don't have to come in," Creed begins. "This won't be pretty."

"I need to," I tell him, gripping his arm, "I have to see it finished."

He nods and we get out of the car, hand in hand walking into the house I grew up in.

One of them must have knocked Dean out along the way, he is slumped over in the chair they have him tied to, with plastic lining the floors.

Creed strips off his button down, leaving him in his t-shirt, God, I thought he was hot before, but seeing him completely zoning into his element is fucking off the charts hot. Luca finds me a seat and places the chair at the corner of the plastic. Not close enough to be sprayed with blood, but close enough I can watch everything.

"Wake him up," Creed commands, "I want him alert to feel everything I do to him, and I want him to know my wife watched me do it all."

They pour ice water on him, the man with the bubbly scar, and Nile. Jarring Dean from unconsciousness.

His eyes dart around the room, landing on me.

"Don't look at her," Creed rumbles, "Don't speak to her, don't even think about her. She's mine, and she always will be. She's going to watch as I carve every pound of flesh she's owed from your body."

He laughs, but it isn't like the manic laugh from before.

This one is something altogether new, as if he doesn't care if he's going to be ripped apart.

Creed grabs a pair of pliers from a table set up off to the side of the room. He grips Dean's tied hands and maneuvers the pliers to grasp a nail. Ripping one off, Dean howls, but Creed continues until he has finished with one hand.

Dean is still screaming.

Creed moves onto his shoes and takes them off, gripping his toenails with the pliers, he rips those out too. They all go into a jar on the table where Creed switches out his tools. He flips a knife over, the glint pulling Dean's attention.

"No, p-ppp-please," he begs.

"*Now* he wants to beg," Creed mocks, carving a line down the side of Dean's face. He plunges the knife into Dean's shoulder, poking holes into his body, making sure to not hit anything important and cutting his fun short. The sounds coming from Dean are jumbled, but all reek of pain.

Creed is a master with a blade, sawing off chunks of Dean's skin carefully, carving him up like a pumpkin on Halloween. The way he takes care to separate the skin from the muscle, making sure to not cut too deep, lest Dean bleed out and die too soon.

The screams and tears coming from the man who traumatized me, and killed so many of the people I loved are a balm to my soul, and I don't care if that makes me a monster.

He deserves all of it. I want him to feel everything, but he loses consciousness too soon. Creed wipes the blade off on a towel he hung from his belt, and turns to look at me, presumably to make sure I'm alright. I nod and give him a sadistic smile that must shock him because his eyebrows shoot up.

Turning back to his collection of tools he pulls a spiked mallet from the table, swinging it a few times and hitting his palm. The sound of metal hitting his flesh is solid, and I can only hope to guess what he plans to do with it.

One of the men from the restaurant pulls Dean's head up by his hair, ripping the roots and slapping his face to wake him up. He gargles on his words, pleading with Creed to stop. Everything he says falls on deaf ears as Creed makes his instructions clear.

"Hold him," his lips tip up into a wicked smile,."This is going to hurt."

I am right on the edge of my seat, gripping the edge, waiting. Every sound in the room disappears as Creed takes a knife and slices a path across his lap, opening up Dean's pants, straight through to his dick.

Eyeing the room, I see everyone held in Creed's orbit.

He pinches Dean's chin between his fingers and whispers something in his ear before pulling back and swinging the meat tenderizer down on Dean's manhood.

The sound is atrocious, squelching and splatters hit the floor and bits of skin land on Creed's pants as Dean's screams turn to shrieks, before he passes out completely. Creed swings the metal until there's nothing left to swing at. Where his dick and balls once sat is a mess of blood, tissue, and skin.

It should make me sick, I see a few of the men around turning green, and I start to laugh.

It's manic. But I can't stop.

The door bangs open, and in strides an older woman with graying brown hair and strikingly familiar features. She closes the door with a huff and stops, looking over where everyone has paused to stare at her.

Creed smiles, a half smile I've never seen before, "Hello, Gran."

The woman scoffs, fixing him with a hard stare, "You rang darling grandson."

Well, holy shit. He has a grandmother?

"Conall, please tell me what the devil is going on."

Creed's father steps out of the ring of observation crossing the space to kiss her cheeks.

"Lovely as always mother," he snips, "I'll give you the cliff notes while you look at Creed's friend's ankle."

She seems happy with that answer, and follows him over to where Candy and Manson are waiting in my father's old office.

With Gran taken care of, Creed snaps in front of Dean's face, waking him up to continue his payment. I watch as Creed blinds him, growing angrier that every time he wakes up his eyes travel to me.

It makes me happy, knowing he is being tortured in the house he murdered my parents in. Maybe that makes me a little bit fucked up, that I enjoy his pain, but I can't help that it feels good knowing he's getting what he deserves. It goes on for hours, and every time Dean passes out they wait for him to wake back up. Eventually I stand, walking onto the plastic.

Creed swivels his head to me, "I'm tired, can we go home?" I plead.

Dean is nothing more than a bleeding pin cushion with missing teeth, strips of skin sawed off his muscles. I'm tired, and ready to finally end this.

Creed offers me the knife, letting me decide if I want his blood on my hands. I take it, shoving it into his stomach and feeling the effortless way it cuts through his skin and sinew.

The ease in which it takes the knife to sink into his skin.

How serene I feel, having taken his life.

I know, later, I will have to journal this all out. But for now, I'm satisfied.

Together, Creed and I can burn those pieces and let the others fall into place.

ONE

YEAR

LATER

Epilogue

We buried my parents the next day in the field beside Creed's mother. It was a gorgeous summer day, as I watched their caskets being lowered into the ground and covered in dirt.

Creed sat with me the whole time, along with all the men in my house. Diego insisted on coming, even though he had broken ribs and a broken ankle.

He looked like he'd been through hell, but he is a loyal friend, through and through.

Manson held my hand until I let him go. He cried and hugged me to his chest for a long minute before we gave their graves one more look. I knew I would be back, if only to feel close to them.

They would be proud of the woman I have become. That together, with this makeshift new family of mine, I healed. I still have some bad days, but Creed is there, every time I start to spiral.

It has been a year since we buried my parents, and Dean 'disappeared'. The boys went to a fancy new school to finish out their high school days, so the house has been pretty quiet until recently.

They are home for the summer, and for the wedding. Creed proposed in the barn, bringing me to tears and then fucking me against the wall.

The ring was a shock, an emerald cut aquamarine stone with pavè diamonds along the band, white gold, and absolutely perfect. Some days I can't help staring at it.

"You're not dressed yet!" Candy screeches.

My hair and makeup are done, and I am sitting in the lingerie she bought me specifically for tonight. The lace covers and pushes my tits up making them look perky and round, the corset is see through lace, and the thong is bedazzled with one word.

CHARMER

"They can't start without me," I joke.

She snaps her fingers at me, waving her arms like a loon, "come on you gorgeous bitch! Put that dress on."

I smirk but oblige.

It's a simple design as far as wedding dresses go, cream material with a lace patterned overlay. The bodice fits perfectly once Candy zips me up, hugging my breasts tight.

Seeing myself in the sleeveless gown gives me all the butterflies.

The skirt starts at my hips and flares out slightly to the bottom where there is no train. We'd decided the barn would be the perfect place to say the vows we never got to say.

Candy tears up once I spin around and she stands back, "you're stunning."

With a goofy smile I take one long look at myself in the mirror. With my raven locks–that have grown down to my lower back–slightly curled and smoothed over my ears, and my makeup done lightly enough, I still look like me.

"Someone wants to see you," Candy smiles, and opens the door. Noah stands there, smiling wide with his arm looped in Miss Loretta's.

I want to cry, but know if I do I will ruin my carefully crafted makeup, and Candy will be pissed.

I wave my arms inside, beckoning them in. Miss Loretta eases herself onto the sofa with Noah's help and tells me to spin around.

"My God," she declares, "I never thought I'd see the day." Her eyes are teary but her smile lights up her whole face.

"I owe you a lot of the credit," I sit between them, grabbing their hands, "to both of you."

"You've made incredible progress," Noah nudges my shoulder.

Looking at Candy, I beam, "I've had a lot of help."

Working at Candy's bakery is one of the things that helped, especially when Creed was gone. Gretchen had to be replaced after she was found dead in her car the night after we handled Dean.

"That's good," he nods, "you look beautiful, Creed's a lucky man."

"No doubt about that," Candy laughs, "now, Miss Loretta, Noah, we have a bride to get married off."

"Save me a dance?" Noah asks, helping Miss Loretta up and they travel down to the patio where Mack has a golf cart waiting for them so Miss Loretta doesn't have to walk.

I watch them from the window of my room, feeling a sense of gratitude. My parents aren't here to see me marry Creed, but everyone else is, and that will have to be okay.

I have no doubt that my parents are watching as I walk down the stairs where Creed's dad waits.

He offered to walk me down the aisle, not out of pity, but love. I have grown close to Conall, he flies down every few weeks to stay with us and talk business with Creed. But he always makes time to hang out with me.

"You're the most exquisite bride I've ever seen, Fern," he

kisses my cheek and takes my arm. I can't wait to see the barn decorated, the butterflies in my stomach take off when Candy walks out to tell them I'm ready.

"I'm nervous," I admit. Not because Creed is waiting for me, but because of all the people who are here, "there's a lot of people here."

"They're all a bunch of babies, wait until you see them cry," he winks and I giggle.

Candy sends Conall the all clear and we head to the golf cart waiting by the back patio. He drives us carefully down to the barn where double doors have been closed at the beginning of the aisle.

I can't see anything, other than a few guests who are sitting in the wooden chairs near the doors. Conall helps me out of the cart and hooks his arm through mine at the doors.

Taking a deep breath, I wait for them to open.

Both doors swing wide, and hot damn, the barn was transformed into a magical glowing scene.

String lights run from the front doors to the back of the barn, lighting up the whole building. The doors at the back of the barn are thrown open behind where Creed is standing, and I can see Daisy and Rambow's heads peeking out of their stalls.

Everyone is dressed in either black or white, and finally as the music begins to play softly in the background, he turns around, waiting at the end of the aisle in black slacks and a white button up.

His eyes latch onto mine, and I swear I see them water. Conall and I make our way to where Creed stands with the officiant, all my nerves go out the window when he mouths 'I love you'. The crowd of people fades away the closer I get to him.

When we get to the front the officiant asks, "who gives this bride to this man?"

"I do, on behalf of her father, rest his soul." Conall states.

Creed takes my hand as I stand across from him, I stare at this impossibly strong man who would do anything to make me happy.

Even wear a tie.

His wavy hair is tied up in a knot on the crown of his head, his beard trimmed and he has never looked more handsome.

The officiant starts the ceremony, and we exchange rings and vows.

"You may kiss the bride," he says and Creed wastes no time, cupping the side of my face with one hand and sliding his other onto my neck, his lips meet mine.

He takes his time, ignoring the hoots and hollers of guests.

It's just us in that moment, the two of us basking in each other's gravity. I didn't think I would ever get to have this, but he promised me, and he never breaks his promises.

When we part, he rests his forehead against mine, "I love you, so much."

"I love you too," I whisper and the cheers continue as we walk, hand in hand, down the aisle.

Wondering how Creed felt that Halloween night? Read on, for an exclusive peek into his head.

Bonus Chapter

Creed

I spot her before she sees me, and *goddamn*, she's a sight. The way the orange material clings to her hips, and flares just so. I have to bite my tongue and tear my eyes away from her.

Snake Charmer.

That's what she is, what she's always been. I've called her Charmer for years, never explaining why. Being older than her, it would be hard to explain without sounding like a total fucking creep.

Even though I'm beginning to think, for her, I'll be anything… everything.

Manson already found me, telling me about Candy being here with some frat dude she recently met. Which is what set me on edge, if Candy is here, Fern is here. In a scantily clad inmate costume no less.

She has me hard just standing there, stretched up on her toes, elongating her thick legs, searching through the fridge for water. I sense it the moment she clocks me. The way her body stiffens and then melts into a comfortable playfulness.

A drunk idiot cat calls out to her again, and I have to hold my fists in an iron grip so I don't throttle him. I'm not very good with words when it comes to her.

"You shouldn't be here," I rumble and follow her out the back door, where more college idiots are exhaling smoke into the sky.

"Last time I checked, I didn't need your permission to do anything."

She spins around with her sassy comment and plants her hands on her wide hips.

"Where are your clothes, Charmer?" I can't help but look my fill, the way her stomach dips and softens with every breath she takes.

"I'm wearing them," she spins, flaring the skirt so I get a glimpse of her perfectly plump ass. An ass that only I should be seeing... or at least that's what my mind keeps telling me. I rip my jacket off quickly, holding it out for her to take.

"Put it on, or I'll put it on for you."

She crosses her arms and stomps her foot, like I figured she would, and fuck me if it doens't turn me on.

"I think I'll pass, thank you."

She passes me, and I black out for a moment. Gripping her hair by the sleek ponytail she styled... I warned her. Being able to anticipate her movements is the highlight of any of our sparring matches. She spins around, presumably to light into me, but I don't give her the chance.

I slide the sleeves over her arms and zip up the jacket that hangs off her body, clearly a size or two too big, "I warned you."

The sky opens up with a loud crack, and rain begins pelting down around us. I don't think as I gently grasp her arm, pulling her close and maneuvering us to where Manson and I parked Dean's car.

Opening the passenger door, I place her on the seat, and walk around the front opening it and sliding into the driver's seat.

"Candy," she starts.

"Manson already found her, how do you think I knew to look for you?" It isn't a complete lie, Manson had found Candy before I found Fern. Even though I felt my skin heat long before Manson told me.

I turn the engine over, letting it run for a moment before reversing the car out and onto the road. My mind keeps envisioning her, legs spread open, teasing me as I try like hell to be a gentleman.

"You look good tonight, Charmer."

Fuck me, well, there's that. I catch her eye roll, and curse myself for speaking and making this situation worse.

When I safely get her to the gates of her house, I find an umbrella in Dean's car and pop it open. Following behind her so she won't get any more wet than she already is. My mind conjures images it shouldn't, about Fern being wet.

"I can hold my own fucking umbrella," she argues.

I want to laugh, but instead reply with, "well aware, but maybe you could let me be a gentleman for once."

At the door I lean down into her space to smell her shampoo, willing her to protest, or make a barb at my comment, or maybe push me away

She surprises me by colliding against my mouth. Eyes wide open, and brain short-circuting, I stand there, like a fucking fool. When my stupid body catches up with what is happening, I back her up against the door and pin her there with my body as I let my lips move against hers.

My hands go to her waist, and I squeeze her body.

She gasps, and I reluctantly pull my lips from hers, laying my forehead against her hair. I take a deep breath and turn away to get back in the car and return to the party.

Fuck.

I shouldn't have kissed her. I should have waited, God, I'm an idiot for sticking around after dropping her off.

Manson will have my head if he finds out.

There are people I need to speak with, things I have to do before I can claim her as mine.

And I will, as soon as I can. My thoughts drift in and out as I make my way back to the party to pick up Manson and Candy. I need to tell him what happened, explain.

When I get there Manson is waiting, depositing a fuming Candy in the back seat. She's yelling about something, a guy maybe, I can't focus because all I can think about is the way Fern's lips molded to mine.

The way *she* kissed *me*.

As soon as I pull into the Hayes's driveway–for the second time tonight– Candy bolts before I even put the car in park.

"Man," Manson pauses holding the car handle. His voice pulls me out of my fog.

"You staying tonight?" He asks.

I nod, because I can't go home to an empty house. Where the smell of my mother lingers and the memory of Fern's kiss burns on my lips.

Wrong.

She would have loved Fern. I know she did, even in the few times she met her. But to know that I love her, and that one day, she will love me too...I would kill to be able to tell my mom.

Sometimes after Fern would blow through from time to time, I would catch my mother smiling after her, as if she knew that Fern would be the woman for me. It's that memory that I try to hold on to.

Manson snores while hanging off the edge of the bed. His breaths are long and loud. I was kidding myself when I though I was getting any sleep tonight with that fucking kiss replaying in my head.

That's how I find myself sitting outside of Fern's room, listening to her and Candy blabber on about how much of a pain in the ass Manson and I are.

It makes me chuckle quietly to myself.

Oh, Charmer. Complain all you want, but I know your dirty little secret.

You want me, just as much as I want you.

And I'll make you mine, if it's the last thing I do.

Acknowledgements

Here we are!!

You made it!!

This book was a passion project, something that I started for shits and giggles. Fern came to me panicked and scared, and I knew then, that I had to write her story. Then Creed popped up, and whew, did we go places. I hope you enjoyed their story, I know I did while writing it.

I have so many people to thank.

Trinity, my editor, my-well, everything. You always know when to push me into writing a little more. To bring my willy-nilly brain back down to earth. It's a job in itself. I don't know how you do it. But, I sure am glad you do. I wouldn't be as confident in publishing this passion project without your guidance and keen eye. You make me a better author with every project we work on.

Ashley, thank you for pushing me as I wrote this story. Your shared love for slashers is written in every word in this story, and I hope I made you proud. Thank you for proofreading, and being there when I have a meltdown.

Tina, thank you for always being there to find my plot holes and missing punctuation. You have no idea the amount of thanks I have for you. I can't imagine writing a book without you pulling my thoughts together.

Jess, thank you for always being the ultimate hype woman! I know you're always down to read anything I write, even if it's shit. I can!t wait for you to read this one.

To all of my street team, thank you for being so excited about my books. It's a wild feeling, and I hope I never take it for granted. If I do, just smack some sense into me.

;P

Finally, to my readers, thank you times A MILLION! None of my books would be possible without y'all reading and reviewing my stories. I hope you know just how much I adore each and every one of you!

About the Author

Taylor Wilson-West is a firm believer that the magic of words on a page can transport readers to new places, and finds comfort in making new, albeit fictional, friends. Currently residing in a small town in North Carolina with her husband and two perfect kiddos, she lives off Cheerwine, potatoes, and ranch dressing. When she's not reading or writing, she can be found shopping at bookstores, adding to her never ending bookshelves. Taylor finds it necessary to have a bookish candle that fits every genre and book character that she has ever fallen in love with. Her favorite moment in any consumable media is when confident, fat main characters get their happily ever after.

If you've made it this far, please leave a review! Reviews are an author's best friend, and readers obviously! :P

<u>GoodReads</u>

<u>Amazon</u>

Find me here:

Instagram